Ali Lutfi Abdallah was born in Rufaa and educated in Bakhtarruda on the White Nile and Britain. He has spent his life teaching in Saudi Arabia, Sudan, and the United States. **Kate Harris** was born in New York City and educated in California and upstate New York. She works as an editor in Atlanta. **Elnour Hamad** was born in Sudan. He works as a painter, illustrator, and an editorial cartoonist in Illinois.

THE CLEVER SHEIKH OF THE BUTANA

AND OTHER STORIES

SUDANESE FOLK TALES

Retold by
Ali Lutfi Abdallah

Illustrated by
Elnour Hamad

Edited by
Kate W. Harris

With an introduction by
W. Stephen Howard

INTERLINK BOOKS
NEW YORK

First published 1999 by

INTERLINK BOOKS
An imprint of Interlink Publishing Group, Inc.
99 Seventh Avenue • Brooklyn, New York 11215 and
46 Crosby Street • Northampton, Massachusetts 01060

Library of Congress Cataloging-in-Publication Data

Abdallah, Ali Lutfi.
The clever sheikh of the Butana and other stories : Sudanese folk tales / retold
by Ali Lutfi Abdallah ; edited by Kate W. Harris ; illustrated by Elnour Hamad.
p. cm.
ISBN 1-56656-312-7 (pbk.)
1. Tales—Sudan. I. Harris, Kate W. II. Title.
GR355.8.A24 1999
398.2'09624—dc21   99–21085
CIP

Printed and bound in Canada
10 9 8 7 6 5 4 3 2 1

To order or request our complete catalog,
please call us at **1-800-238-LINK** or write to:
Interlink Publishing
46 Crosby Street, Northampton, MA 01060
e-mail: interpg@aol.com • website: www.interlinkbooks.com

CONTENTS

ACKNOWLEDGMENTS

The most important reason for my visit to America, after seeing my sons and relatives here, was to try to raise funds to establish Lutfi University in Rufa'a Town in the Sudan. My father, Sheikh Lutfi, opened an intermediate school there, which became a secondary school in 1945. My brothers, sisters, and I are now trying to make it into a university.

To that end, Ms. Martty Berner, a dear friend, suggested that I retell these stories and offered to transcribe them from the audio cassettes on which I recorded them. Before traveling to Eritrea, she typed the first batch of stories. To her I extend my deepest thanks.

I would also like to thank my daughter, Nafiesa, and her husband, Ali, for typing some of the stories. Dr. Dale and Connie Gephart gave very useful suggestions and tried their best to find a publisher and an editor.

My thanks to the principal, assistant principal, and teachers of Attwood School in Fort Worth, Texas, for reading the stories, and allowing me to read them, to all the students of the school. Their comments were of great value.

I would also like to thank many of the students of the Fort Worth Independent School District for the encouraging comments they sent after reading some of the stories with my elder brother, their teacher, Yousif Lutfi Abdalla. I received many letters from these young people, and am grateful for each one.

The suggestions of Professor Martin Dali played a major role in the development of this book.

Thanks also go to my brother-in-law, Dr. Kamal el-Hadi, who corrected errors in the text and offered many helpful suggestions.

All of these people, and others not mentioned here, helped me greatly as I prepared the stories to send to my dear friend, Professor Abdullahi Ahmed An-Na'im, who introduced me and the stories to his friend, Kate W. Harris. She edited all the stories and found a publisher.

My deep thanks also to my friend, Professor Stephen Howard, for his welcoming introduction. His love of the Sudan and his wonderful words add so much to the book.

The beautiful illustrations of my dear friend, Elnour Hamad, add to the Sudanese flavor of the stories. To him my deep thanks for his efforts and encouragement.

With the help of all these good people, these stories are now available for American readers. To all I extend my sincere thanks and friendship. Lastly, I thank the publisher for bringing these Sudanese stories, and the culture and values they carry with them, to my American friends. Between the lines of these stories appear the great, faithful, generous, brave people of my beloved Sudan.

INTRODUCTION
RETOLD TALES FROM SUDAN
by W. Stephen Howard

The red globe of the sun rules the landscape that is the setting for these Sudanese stories retold by Ali Lutfi. The sun colors the clay cracking soil, grows the palm trees bright green, and bleaches the cotton white. Where blue sky joins the Blue Nile river running ochre with silt borne from Ethiopia's highlands is a place where stories—for learning, entertaining, and spiritual guidance—have been told for centuries. This landscape, marked by steep river banks, low brush, small red clay brick villages, and the criss-cross of irrigation canals, is dun and blue, a drab backdrop for these vivid tales. And the tough terrain—the heat, the dust—provides drama enough for any story-teller, let alone a storyteller with ties to the cultures that arose from this place.

Ali Lutfi has retold tales from the cultures of Northern, Eastern, and Central Sudan, part of the vast territory in this, the largest country in Africa. The name Sudan, which comes from the ancient Arabic term for the region—*bilad as-Sudan,* or "land of the blacks"—is a crossroads of peoples and cultures. Arabs from the North and East, African pilgrims from the West en route to Mecca, and ancient migrations of Africans from the South, have settled and intermarried with the original inhabitants of the Nile Valley over the millennia. But the origins of the "Sudanese" is a subject of some controversy. On the one hand are those who for various political reasons wish to connect themselves with the "Arab East." On the other is the evolving alternative discourse that centers on the "African-ness" of the Sudanese and considers the Arab element to be a later layer of their culture.

Today there is an uneasy coexistence among these diverse peoples and traditions. But the most significant efforts at establishing peace have always centered around the shared elements of regional culture. Which cultural aspects will prevail has been the contentious question, while the stories told herein blend those cultures in a natural way.

The teller of the tales in this book, *Ustadh,* or "teacher," Ali Lutfi, grew up in the small Eastern Gezira town of Rufa'a. The Gezira, "peninsula" in Arabic, referring to the land between the White and Blue Niles, is a fertile region that is the main agricultural resource of Sudan. Cotton is grown for commercial export, and a variety of crops for national consumption and family subsistence are cultivated here. Rufa'a, on the east bank of the Blue Nile, is just outside of the Gezira area, but has a long agricultural tradition of its own. It is easily reachable by canoe or ferry from the west bank of the Blue Nile and serves as a kind of "gateway" to the *butana* or plain referred to in the stories to follow. So Rufa'a itself is a transitional point in the regional cultures, with sedentary agriculturalists and fishing people hugging the Blue Nile's banks, and people with recent pastoral traditions living to the east of town.

Ustadh Ali grew up in a small village called Deim Lutfi, named after his father, a well-known religious and educational leader. Deim ("settlement" or "camp") Lutfi sits between the Blue Nile and the larger town of Rufa'a and is a community of a few large families and the schools that have been an important part of their twentieth century history. Deim Lutfi is uniquely a village of farmer-teachers, with many of its inhabitants serving at one time or another—or at the same time—as teachers and as farmers.

The houses in Deim Lutfi are all made of the red clay bricks that are manufactured by hand at the river's edge. Buildings are close together in the village with a narrow dirt path running between the houses. The climate of Sudan dictates that much of a person's day is spent outside in the shade, so most of the houses are in fact large walled compounds with one- or two-room buildings in the middle. Chairs and beds are moved around the compound, chasing the shaded breezes, as the day wears on. In the hottest weather cooking might be done under a reed lean-to, propped up against a proper kitchen.

In the story-listening days of Ali Lutfi's childhood, Rufa'a and Deim were yet to be electrified. The nights were moonlit or starlit and children were calmed down for sleep by the telling of stories. Or perhaps one of the wedding tales presented here would be told to keep the children busy at the time of a marriage. The old women of the community were the lending libraries for these stories, remembering and embellishing as their energy permitted or as the children's restlessness demanded. Ali recalls that the stories were often told around supper as the children ate a sorghum or millet porridge from one large pot. These story-telling grandmothers were usually illiterate themselves, women's education becoming a priority only recently in Sudan's history. But as is characteristic of an oral society, their memories served to preserve ancient traditions. Older women are often a conservative force in this culture as well, in that they conserve the values which they were taught as girls. The reader will note that in virtually all of the stories in this collection, there is a strong moral message, delivered in an entertaining way to make it easy to remember.

It is important that Ali Lutfi remembers the women who told him these stories for women are essentially relegated to the fringes of Sudan's society. With these tales we observe a realm of women's influence and participation that they could use to inject *their* moral position into the social mix. And the children would absorb the messages—such as the importance of forgiveness central to several of these stories, or an idealized view of humanity that provides a model—in an enjoyable way. The teller would patch the stories from other stories that she had heard, snippets of conversation—perhaps about farming problems in the family, fiercely-held values, and impressions from the limited travels that she had had outside of the family compound. And there is art here as well: the stories set mood, introduce strong characters, develop plots, and are filled with irony.

It is not hard to imagine the small rituals that accompany the telling of the stories. Before she begins her tales, the old woman moves slowly to the *zir*, the clay water jar, for a cup of cool water. She keeps it at her side and sips from it to relieve her dry throat while the children interact with the story with their comments and questions.

Ali Lutfi and siblings and cousins sit around a tray filled with breads and sauces. The woman who made the food is also storyteller, so, in a sense, her retelling the tale is a form of relaxation. She got up at dawn, to say her prayers and then make tea for the family. She helped dress the boys in their simple *ghumsan* (long shirts) before they went off to school, and possibly even made their shirts herself. While telling the tales she employs all manner of linguistic devices to help paint a picture for the children. The visual substitute for those of us reading the stories in English are the drawings of Elnour Hamad, also a son of the Gezira.

If we were able to hear the stories being told, the storyteller would draw out syllables to emphasize size, danger, distance. She would say for example, *kabiiiiiiiir,* for "big" or *baiiiiiiiiid* for "far," stressing with the vowel the enormity of something or someone. The Sudanese love to argue and another linguistic device built into the telling of stories is the debate or conversation that can take place between teller and listener. Many of today's politicians in Sudan first learned to make a point while listening to their grandmothers' stories, although it is probably not appropriate to blame what passes for political discourse in Sudan today on the poor grandmothers!

In any case, the notion of *performance* in oral literature should be noted, that the storyteller will tell her tale differently each time depending on the audience and/or the specific point that she wishes to make with the story. Think about telling a sad story like "The Wicked Brother," with a storm raging outside and maybe adding a few lines to the song verses that we find here. Everyone sitting around the teller knows the outcome; the pleasure is in the telling. Story-tellers gain a reputation for their facility with a tale and many members of the audience will be back to hear the same story again and again. The telling of tales is participatory; the teller takes cues from the audience and the story then lives on with that particular audience's mark upon it. Because teller and listeners are often intimates, the teller can personalize the tale for the specific audience or event around which the story is told. It is appropriate that Ali Lutfi has presented us with a *collection* of stories here, for that is how they are generally recounted. He has filled them, even in English translation, with wonderful expressions from Sudanese Arabic, my favorite being "eyes like cups."

A dominant but not exclusive social force in Northern Sudan is the Islamic faith, which finds an important place in these stories. Islam came to this part of the Nile Valley, displacing Christianity and non-monotheistic religions, around the turn of the 15th–16th centuries. Certainly conquest ensured the dominance of the newcomer Islam in the region, but the faith was also sustained by a steady stream of holy men or teachers who had studied and memorized the Qur'an and who taught the holy scripture to the communities through which they passed. These holy men were often called "sufis" and adhered to the mystical aspect of Islam. Their rituals, often expressed in poetry or *qasida,* spoke lovingly to God and often revealed the religion's connection to nature—God as embracing night or a whispering heart, for example. The tombs of these holy men and women dot the Gezira and hometowns of both Ali Lutfi and the illustrator, Elnour Hamad. The faithful visit the tombs to show respect for those who have walked God's path before us, who can still show us how to stay on that path today.

A glance at a map will indicate the proximity of Sudan to Islam's first place of revelation in Mecca on the Arabian peninsula, just across the Red Sea. Islam, along with Judaism and Christianity, is one of the great monotheistic religions, centering on a belief in one God. Adherents of Islam, called Muslims, also believe in the Prophecy of Mohammed, to whom God revealed Islam's sacred words, the Qur'an, in the seventh century. Memorization of all or some of the Qur'an's verses and their use in daily prayer are the central practiced rituals of the Islamic faith. Some learn the verses by hearing them spoken over and over again, others by intense study. The connections between the tales retold here and Islamic society in Northern Sudan are very deep. We can see the connection in peoples' names, in mentions of breaking the day for prayer, in the role played by religious authorities like *sultans* and *sheikhs.*

But religion is only a part of the purpose of these tales. They can be read on so many levels, reader and teller adding their own layers of meaning. Tales are for enjoyment, to pass the time, to calm restless children, to deliver moral messages, to build solidarity and defuse tensions among peoples and ethnic groups, to explain our origins and heritage and to explain why we are the way we are. "You children are quarreling because you do not know how connected you are; let me tell you a story about our family."

Like virtually all of the lands of Africa, Sudan suffered and survived a series of colonial experiences. In the early 19th century, the Nile Valley of Sudan was ruled by the Ottoman Turks. In the late 19th century, the British conquered most of the country, ruling in a condominium arrangement with Egypt until political independence for Sudan in 1956. In between the Turks and the British, much of Sudan was ruled by an indigenous leader, Mohammed Ahmed El Mahdi, who tried to impose his religious vision on the diverse peoples of Sudan, sometimes ruthlessly. The many and varied cultures of Sudan have thus not been brought to live together under peaceful circumstances, but have rather been incorporated into one state either for colonial expedience or through a dominating religious agenda. Lack of internal integration and frequent turmoil in all of the bordering countries—Egypt, Libya, Chad, Central African Republic, Congo, Uganda, Kenya, Ethiopia, and Eritrea—make for a volatile political situation.

The primary tragedy of this history is the enduring conflict between the northern and southern parts of Sudan. The vast majority of people in the North are Muslim while most people in the South are Christian or practitioners of African religions, but the conflict goes beyond the obvious religious and cultural differences. The South has long been a source of Sudan's human, mineral, and agricultural wealth and the merchants and governments of the North have sought to control these resources and impose their authority over the isolated peoples in the southern region. War continues to rage today between North and South, and the death toll since the 1950s is in the millions from war and resulting famines. Political solutions have been negotiated over the years, but always seem to break down when issues of Southern autonomy are raised.

The reteller of these tales, Ali Lutfi, had his formal education under the British, doing his school studies in the English language. He became a primary school teacher and school inspector in the Gezira area, serving in this capacity for many years under the government of an independent Sudan. He was also involved with both traditional Sufi sects and progressive social movements. The illustrator, Elnour Hamad, studied art at the Khartoum Polytechnic and worked as a teacher of art in secondary schools in Sudan and Oman. Sudan is presently ruled by an intolerant regime guided by its own version of Islam which has little room for democratic visions. Driven into exile for his leadership in a progressive Islamic reform movement, Elnour has had many exhibitions of his artwork and is currently studying for a Ph.D. in Art Education at the University of Illinois.

The stories and illustrations presented here are rich with detail of life in Sudan. *The Fatal Beauty of Tajouj*, for example, is a story usually set in the region of Kassala, and in it we see the value of modesty. The story of Tajouj was the basis for one of the few films made in Sudan in the early 1980s. Other stories, like *In Unity There is Strength*, have familiar themes and are retold here in the context of securing loyalties within large families.

Making these tales of Sudan accessible to an audience in the West is an important step in bringing us closer to an understanding of the foundation of Sudan's culture and of the violent changes that cloud Sudan's present. How will these changes be interpreted by future storytellers? The search for meaning in the world around us, and weaving that meaning into a story for others to listen to, is a task that we all share.

W. Stephen Howard, Ph.D. is Associate Professor and Director of African Studies at Ohio University. He has spent several years teaching, researching, and listening to stories in Sudan.

A FRIEND IN NEED

A very rich Sudanese, who was called Falih, had one son called Najih. Falih was a wise merchant. He was always thinking, and he tried his best to bring up his son to be a young merchant who is aware of what is going on. He brought Najih up in this way, so that his son could carry on his work after him. He looked upon him and thought of him as a progressive young merchant.

One day Falih gave his son quite a large amount of money. He said, "Now, my son, you are old enough to start your own enterprise. Take this money and buy anything you want. Purchase wisely. Use it with good sense and good judgment."

Najih took the money. He began imitating his father, and what his father did. He left the house early each day and returned late in the evening. That went on for some months.

One day Najih asked his father to give him some more money. When Falih asked about the money he had given Najih previously, how it had been spent or what Najih had bought with it, his son answered that he had bought a friend with that money. Falih was very pleased with his son and so he gave him another large sum of money.

Months passed and Najih asked his father for more money. Falih wanted to know where the other money had gone. "What happened to the money I gave you recently?" he asked.

Najih told his father, "I have bought another friend with the money. Now I have two faithful friends." So Falih gave his son money again.

"Now, my son, be very careful and whatever you do with the money, do it wisely. Do things that you will never be sorry you have done. If you need any help I am always ready to help you. Allah bless you," said the father.

Days, weeks, and months went by, and then Najih came to his father for more money. That was the fourth time in just one and a half years. He had bought another friend. His father asked him to wait until nightfall. When night came, Falih slew a sheep. In the dark of night he put the sheep in a sack and put the sack on their donkey's back. Then he and his son went out.

They went to Najih's first friend. Falih stood with the donkey at a distance, where he could hear, and told his son what to say to his friend. Najih knocked at his friend's door. After some time the friend came and opened the door. He was very pleased to find Najih. He invited him to come in, but Najih did not. He said to his friend, "I am in trouble. I am in a very critical situation. I need your help, because you are my oldest and best friend. I can't ask the help of any other but you. Please do your best to help me."

His friend was about to fly with pleasure. He was always waiting for a chance to repay his friend's good deeds toward him. So he replied, "Oh! So at last my chance comes to show my affection for you and try to do something good for you. I am ready to do anything you ask me. You order and I shall obey. What is it that you want me to do? What is this critical situation you are in?"

Najih answered, "I have killed a man. I have put him in a sack on the back of the donkey under that tree. I want you to go with me to the graveyard, help me dig a grave, and bury the body there before daylight, before I can be seen."

Now the friend became very uneasy. He was awkward and embarrassed, especially after talking a lot about his faithfulness and allegiance. This was a different matter. This was very difficult to deal with. He answered, "I am very ill now. I can't go out at all, especially in this cold weather. The doctor told me to stay in bed and not to move or things will be worse for me. I can give you my spade, but I am very sorry. I can't do you any favor at this time except to give you the spade. Do you want it or not? I have to go inside, because of the chill."

Najih refused the spade, thanked his friend, and went away. He told his father of the friend's reply. Then they went to the second friend. Falih, holding the donkey under a tree by the street, waited for his son to ask this friend. When Najih knocked at the door, his friend opened it. He was also pleased to find Najih, and to hear that Najih needed his help. He was always enthusiastic and eager to try to help Najih, who was always doing helpful things for him. But when Najih told him of his need, the friend's face changed. He looked as if he was going to faint. That was not what he had expected. He did not want to help bury somebody. So he said, "You know I am very weak. I cannot hold a spade or carry a dead body. I can help you in any other way but this. Will you accept my apology? I will do any other thing that my health can tolerate or endure, but I cannot do this. I am very sorry."

Najih thanked his friend and accepted his apology. Then he went to tell his father the outcome. Both Falih and Najih went to the third friend. Again the father stood at a distance and Najih knocked at his friend's door. When the friend was told about the crime and Najih's need for his help, he began to tremble, shaking from head to foot. He said to Najih, "You see, I am always afraid to visit the graveyard by day. So I cannot go there by night. I'll die of fright. There is my servant. I may order him to go with you, and help you. He is a very strong man, and never afraid of anything. He is very faithful and will tell nobody. If that is all right, I shall awaken him now."

Najih refused the servant's help, thanked his friend, and went to tell his father the result. All three friends on whom he had spent the money had proved to be unfaithful and useless. He could not count on any of them.

The father said to his son, "I have got a friend and a half. Let us test both my friend, and my half friend, so that we will know if they are sincere or not. Let us first go to the half friend."

It was just before dawn. Najih held the donkey at a distance, and his father knocked at the half friend's door. The man was very surprised to see his friend at his door so early in the morning. He wanted to know the reason for the early visit. Falih said, "A man jumped over my wall. He tried to steal my safe. We fought and the thief has been killed. I want you to help me bury him."

The half friend accepted the task. He said to Falih, "You just go to your house. I will bury the dead man myself. I do not want anyone to see you at the graveyard so early."

Falih thanked his half friend, and told him that he was teaching his son and wanted to show him true friendship. He went to his son, and made sure he had heard every word that was said between his father and his half friend.

Next they went to the full friend to put him to the same difficult test. Again the boy stood at a distance, from which he could hear every word. Falih knocked at the door, just when the cocks were crowing for the dawn prayer. His friend came to the door, opened it, and found his friend, Falih. He was astonished.

"Good morning, friend Falih. What brings you here at this early hour? It must be a significant matter," said the friend.

Falih answered, "I have killed Ali. I have put his body in a sack on my donkey. My son Najih is holding the donkey, waiting for us. I urgently need you to help me bury the body in the graveyard."

The friend replied, "You have not killed Ali. I have killed him. You had nothing to do with it. This is my problem."

Falih said that he had killed Ali. His friend insisted that he himself had committed the crime. He was firmly determined in the matter.

People were coming out of their houses and going to the mosque for the dawn prayer. Falih and his friend were arguing and quarreling about who had killed Ali. The people who were going to the mosque for their prayer heard the two friends quarreling and shouting. They went to them. They asked what the matter was. Each of the two friends told them that he had killed Ali and the other had nothing to do with Ali's death. Each of them said that the people should not believe the other, but believe him alone.

A man stepped from the group and asked them, "Whom did you kill?" Both of them answered at the same time, "I have killed Ali." The man said to them, "I am Ali, and I was not killed by either of you. What is the matter with you two?"

After the prayer Falih stood up and told the people about his son's and his experiments with their friends. And then he reminded the people of the old proverb: A friend in need is a friend indeed.

THE FACE IS A DAGGER

Adaroab was a young man. He was very poor, but he was brave, strong, and generous. He was known for his intelligence and for the fact that nobody had ever heard him tell a lie. He was from the brave Bija tribe, in the eastern part of the Sudan. He lived in Matateib village.

Because he was poor, he used to travel far from his village to work. He would take his sickle and travel to the town of Kassala on the River Gash and find work in the plantations there. After two or three months, he would return to Matateib carrying with him what he bought for his household: coffee beans, sugar, dates, clothes, shoes, and so on.

His young son and two daughters were always with him when he was in the village.

Adaroab was the poorest man in the village. He had only one cow, while other men had at least three cows, and some as many as sixty. He depended on the milk of his cow when he was at Matateib. When he was away the family depended on that beloved cow.

His longest stay with his family would come when he returned in July; he wouldn't go on his journey again before the end of November. In July the rains begin to fall and Adaroab would sow his grain on his small plantation. By the end of November the crop would be harvested.

Between planting the seeds and gathering the crops, the growing sorghum plants were called by many names according to their age and size. When the first leaves came up from the ground, they looked very much like the ears of mice, so the plant was called mouse's ear.

5

Then it became a chick, a chicken, a hen, an eagle, *lateiba* (about to be pregnant), pregnant, *sharaia* (full of immature seeds), "milky" (adolescent, with a milky coating), *fareek* (ripe, but not strong), and when the seeds were strong and ready to be harvested they were called *gawa* (grain).

Those were, and are, the names of the plants from the moment they appeared until the time they were harvested. Those were the best months for farmers.

After the harvest, people sold part of their grain. Marriages usually took place after selling the crops, because people then had money to pay for the marriages.

When Adaroab harvested his crop, he sold part of it, then dug a hole in front of his house and put the rest of the crop into the hole to be prepared for a time of need. He left two or three sacks for the use of his family, then took his sickle and went to Kassala again. Time after time, year after year, he did the same.

Once, when he had been in Kassala for two months, he began to have bad dreams. Every night he dreamed such terrible dreams that he was certain a catastrophe had taken place at home. So he obtained permission from the owner of the plantation on which he was working, and traveled to Matateib.

Arriving home just before sunset, he was met with pleasure by his household. After the *Marhrib* (sunset prayer) he waited for his supper, which was usually bread and milk. The bread was served, but instead of milk there was honey. He liked honey very much.

After supper he asked for a gourd of milk, but his wife told him that there was no milk. When he asked why, she told him that the cow had been eaten by a fierce lion.

Early the next morning all the people of the village came to greet him. They all said they were sorry about what had happened to his cow.

He learned that his cow was the only cow that had been eaten. He also learned that the villagers had tried their best to drive away the lion, but they couldn't. It was the fiercest lion that had ever come to the village, and it was still there.

Adaroab complained aloud to everyone that there were people

who had three cows, others who had twenty cows each, and others with more than fifty cows, yet the lion ate the only cow he had, the one on which his family depended.

His eyes became as red as burning coals. He began to shiver from head to toe. He moved toward the wall on which his sword and shield were hanging. He took them and went out asking people where to find the lion.

The villagers tried their best to stop him, because they had gone after the lion before and were almost killed.

But it was as if Adaroab was in another world. He was the most ferocious man ever born. He was as savage as the lion himself.

His only cow! Out of the hundreds of cows owned by the villagers, the rich villagers, the well-to-do! Only his, the cow of the poorest man to be found.

All the villagers were afraid of the lion. In time all their animals would be eaten, and they could do nothing.

Being unable to stop Adaroab, most of the men got their weapons and went to help him. They showed him the thick trees where the lion made his home.

Then Adaroab said, "I will divorce my wife if any one of you comes with me! I will go alone. I will fight the lion alone as long as the lion will fight me alone."

He disappeared among the trees. They heard the lion roar fiercely. The lion roared again and again. Then there was silence, the silence of the grave. Time passed, and nothing happened.

They were now afraid that Adaroab had met his end. They waited for a long time, for what felt like days.

Again the roar of the lion was heard. This was the roar of attack. The lion was charging. Then another roar was heard, but it sounded like a roar of pain. Then silence again.

At dusk they thought they could see something moving toward them. In the twilight they saw Adaroab walking in their direction, pulling the dead lion by his tail.

They all congratulated one another. They approached Adaroab, but he was a different man. His color was reddish, his eyes were like glowing embers, and they were about to pop out of their lids.

His lips were thin and drawn. He shivered all over as if he had malaria. He couldn't talk.

The people carried the dead lion to Adaroab's house, and began to rejoice. When the next day broke, all the men brought tea and breakfast to Adaroab's house. They ate together, enjoying the best of times.

A wise, rich, generous old man said to Adaroab, "We know that you never tell lies. I want to ask you a question and if you answer it truthfully, I will give you three cows and an ox. How did you feel when you met the lion? Were you afraid or not?"

Adaroab answered, "You remember that all of you tried to stop me from going after the lion, but I refused. Truthfully, I was so angry that I was not frightened. But when his eyes met mine, I remembered the proverb, 'The face is a dagger.' Right then, if a small child had tried to stop me from fighting the lion, I would have obeyed him. And, by Allah, if the lion had found an excuse not to fight me, he would have done so."

All the people were glad and Adaroab received his three cows and an ox.

THE STORY OF AL GISEIMA

The forty-three grandsons of the great-grandfather gathered around him and asked him to tell them the story of Al Giseima. The people of the village said that Omer was one hundred and seventy-five years old. But, astonishingly, he was still strong and trying to marry for the sixteenth time, because all his wives had grown old and died a long time ago. They said that his last wife died about fifty years ago.

Omer was in very good condition, still strong and with a clear memory. He forgot nothing of his childhood, boyhood, adolescence, or adulthood. He traveled a lot, visiting hundreds of villages and cities, because he was a caravan leader for merchants and traders. He was a merchant himself.

He said to them, "I still remember that all the girls of the village were the most beautiful girls of the country, and Al Giseima was the most beautiful of all of them. We were small children when she was forty years old, but still she was the most beautiful person.

"She was very young when she lost her mother, only six months old. Her grandmother, the mother of her mother, took care of her. She brought her up well. She was a polite girl. She was the best cook of all the girls. In needle work no girl could equal her. She was kind to the poor. She was a perfect girl. All this was told to us by our elders, because we were children.

"Her grandmother always kept her at home, because she reminded her of her daughter, the dead mother of Al Giseima. A brave young man called Wad Annameer was engaged to her. He paid all the money

11

for the marriage which the bride's family had requested.

"They decided that the marriage would be in a year."

⊷═◉═⊷

There were six wicked girls in the village. They envied Al Giseima. They tried their best to cause her trouble, but they couldn't find any chance, because she was sheltered all the time by her grandmother.

One day they went to the grandmother and asked her to allow Al Giseima to go out with them to collect wood, because she had never gone out with them as all the young girls did in that village at that time. They wanted to get to know her better and become good friends.

The grandmother told them that was not her concern, but the concern of the grandfather, who was the father of Al Giseima's father. They approached him, and asked him. He answered that the matter was given to his son, Al Giseima's uncle.

So they went to his son, Al Giseima's uncle, and asked him to permit Al Giseima to go out with them. He delivered the matter to his uncle, his father's brother, to decide whether she would go or not.

They went to the uncle. Her great-uncle said to them, "But Al Giseima grew up in her grandmother's house, so the husband of the grandmother, that is Al Giseima's grandfather, is responsible. Go and see him."

They went to Al Giseima's grandfather, that wise, quiet, and thoughtful man. They tried to obtain permission for Al Giseima to go out with them. After thinking it over, he told them that he would put them to a test, and if they succeeded, he would allow her to go out with them. The girls agreed.

The grandfather brought three sacks: one of corn, one of wheat, and one of rice. He mixed them thoroughly together, poured them on the ground, mixed them with the dust, and asked the girls to put each kind in its sack, without any grain of the others or of the dust. They must complete this in two days' time.

The girls, wishing to cause trouble for Al Giseima, worked very hard on their task. When the time came the sacks were full, with each grain in its own sack.

When the grandfather saw what they had done, he was very pleased. He said, "You are very patient, careful girls. I allow Al Giseima to go out with you."

The next day they went out, taking the innocent Al Giseima with them. She was very pleased to go out. They collected a considerable amount of wood from the forest near the river.

Each girl wore jewels and gold around her neck, and rings around her hands and fingers, because at that time every man bought jewels, gold, and silver for his daughters. Each of the six girls collected her jewelry in a handkerchief and hid it. Each girl had another handkerchief in which she put a stone and tied it well. Then one of the girls said, "Allah curse the girl's father who doesn't throw her jewelry far in the river." Following that, the girl threw the handkerchief in which the stone was tied far into the river. Each of the other five girls followed the first girl's deed and threw the handkerchief in which she had tied the stone.

Al Giseima was surprised, but she remembered that the girl said, "Allah curse the girl's father who doesn't throw her jewels in the river." All the girls had done it. Should only her dead father be cursed by Allah? She would not allow that and be mocked in the village. So she collected all her jewelry, put it in her handkerchief, tied it well and threw it as far as her strength could. Then the girls began to giggle among themselves, pleased at being able to deceive her.

As they were returning to the village, they came across a tall date palm, rising up high in the air, as if trying to reach the clouds. It was full of red, ripe, sweet dates. One of the girls said, "Oh! What beautiful and ripe dates! But I can't climb."

Another one said, "Yes, aren't they ready to be eaten? But I can't eat them, because I never learned to climb trees." Each girl said that the dates were sweet, but every one of them said that she didn't know how to climb trees.

Al Giseima said, "Well, I'll climb the tree and throw you the dates, but please collect dates for me as you do for yourselves." She climbed the tree and began to shake the thorny branches, and a lot of dates fell down. Each girl filled her bag with juicy, sweet, ripe dates, but they filled Al Giseima's bag with green rotten dates and tied it for her.

At last, before the sunset, she came down, and they began walking toward the village. One of the girls said, "Allah curse the girl's father who doesn't eat some of her dates." Each girl began to eat the best of the dates in her bag. But Al Giseima found that all the dates that the girls put in her bag were rotten. She got angry, but kept her anger to herself and said nothing.

Another girl said, "Allah curse the girl's father who doesn't put on her jewelry." They took out their handkerchiefs, untied them, and each one of the girls took her jewelry and wore it. At that point Al Giseima knew that her friends had deceived her. She began to weep bitterly. They laughed at her and ran to the village. She returned to the river. She sat there sadly, weeping.

After some time she saw a white wind moving in the sky toward her. All the trees were moving this way and that in the wind. She was afraid. She had never seen such a wind in all her life. She cried, "Allah protect me from that wind." The wind said to her, "Allah protect you from what is following me." Then the wind disappeared beyond the far horizon. There were high waves in the river.

Not long after that a yellow wind appeared in the sky. The trees moved this way and that even more fiercely than the time before. Al Giseima said, "Oh! Allah protect me from that wind." And the wind said to her, "Allah protect you from what is coming after me." The waves were higher than the previous time.

A blue wind appeared after that. Now Al Giseima said, "Oh! Allah save me from that wind. Allah protect me from the blue one."

The blue wind, before disappearing, answered her saying, "Allah save you and protect you from the wind that is coming after me." The waves were still higher.

There, far away, appeared a very black, black wind. The trees were rocking and crying with a fearful noise. The highest branches were about to reach the ground. The trees were about to be pulled from their roots. Al Giseima cried very loudly, "Oh! Allah protect me from the black wind." The black wind said to her, "Allah protect you from what is inside me." Then Al Rhoole climbed down from the wind. (Al Rhoole, as you may know, is wicked, ugly, and causes trouble for people.)

The wind changed into a cyclone, a tornado. It turned round and round and round and went up into the sky and disappeared. Al Rhoole was very ugly. He heard Al Giseima crying. He sniffed and said, "I smell a human being." Sniffing this way and that, looking about, he found Al Giseima. He was amazed to see such beauty. But she was weeping, she was very sad. He asked her the reason for her distress, why she was crying. She told him the whole story.

He said to her, "I can bring you back your jewelry." He began to drink the water in the river. He went on drinking and drinking and drinking. There was less and less water in the river, until it was all drunk by Al Rhoole. There in the empty riverbed was the handkerchief with the jewels. She took it. Al Rhoole opened his mouth and all the water rushed back into its place.

The girls, when they reached the village, lied and said that Al Giseima had gotten lost and that they couldn't find her. Al Giseima didn't come back for weeks. The people looked everywhere for her, but they found nothing except her tracks and the tracks of Al Rhoole. They were sure that Al Rhoole had eaten her. So they wept for her, and there was the house of mourning for seven days.

Wad Annameer was absent. He was away collecting money for his marriage, his bride, and to build a beautiful house for both of them. Many months passed and, when he came back, ready for the marriage, Wad Annameer was told what had happened. They told him that Al Rhoole took Al Giseima and ate her. He couldn't believe it.

He went to a carpenter and asked him to make him the most beautiful gazelle he could make of wood. The carpenter made a most beautiful gazelle. Wad Annameer carried his wooden gazelle from village to village, asking whomever he met, "Have you seen a more beautiful gazelle than mine, than this?" The answer was always, "No." Everybody told him that his gazelle was the most beautiful. He traveled on and on.

Months passed before he came to a far away village. Outside the village was a small house inhabited by a very old woman. He greeted her and she answered and asked him to climb down off his horse and be her guest and eat and drink. So he climbed down. After the meal, he got out his wooden gazelle, and said to the old woman, "Oh grandmother!" (She was not really his grandmother, but in Sudan all old women are called grandmother.) "Have you ever seen a more beautiful gazelle than this?" Strangely enough she answered him that his gazelle was very beautiful, but there was a gazelle that was more beautiful than his.

"What did you say, grandmother?" asked Wad Annameer.

She said to him, "There is a gazelle that is more beautiful than yours. Your gazelle is made of wood, but there is a human gazelle. She is married to Al Rhoole. Her name is Al Giseima."

Wad Annameer now was about to fly, because he was so very glad. He told the old woman all about his sweetheart, Al Giseima.

She said to him, "Well, I'll help you. Take this thorn of the *hijleej* tree, and this stone, and this mud. Take care of these things. Go to the village that you can see from here. That is Al Rhoole's village. If you find him asleep, well and good. You may complete your mission. But if you find him awake, do not enter the village. Al Rhoole is usually awake for a complete year, but he is also asleep for another year."

He asked her, "How do I know whether he is asleep or awake?"

She told him , "If there is smoke reaching to the clouds that means he is awake, because as long as he is awake he is eating. He cooks and cooks and cooks. But if there is no smoke and you hear thunder, that means he is asleep. That thunder is his snoring. Go slowly and you will find that your promised wife has become a Rhoola (a female Rhoole, as mean and ugly and evil as Al Rhoole). Her nose will be long, and she will have big red eyes. Because her hair is very long, Al Rhoole is using it as a cushion under his head.

"Take everything in the house outside, and burn it. Cut her nails and her hair. Don't leave the smallest thing in the house. Make sure that everything is burned."

He went. He was afraid, because he felt the ground shaking under his feet, and heard a loud thunder. That was Al Rhoole's snoring, to his good luck.

When he reached the house, Wad Annameer crept cautiously and entered the room. There he found Al Giseima with very long nails, a long nose, and big red eyes. The first thing he did was to cut her nails.

The moment he did that she was changed, and appeared as she had before, beautiful, mild, and very sweet.

He was ready to take her, but her hair was under Al Rhoole's head. He cut her hair. They both collected everything in the house and burned it. Two things were left unburned: Al Rhoole's *mufraka* (a kitchen tool used for mixing foods) and a big round stone called Al Mungar. Wad Annameer put Al Giseima on his horse's back, rode with her, and the horse flew, carrying them both.

Back in Al Rhoole's house, the *mufraka* entered its master's mouth, nose, and ears, and turned round and round and round to wake Al Rhoole. It sang:

> Oh! Al Rhoole my dear,
> Who sleeps a year,
> Who wakes a year,
> The house mistress was taken away,
> Wake up and move and don't delay,
> Catch him and let him be killed,
> Before your heart with distress is filled.

The Mungar jumped up in the air and fell on Al Rhoole's head. The *mufraka* turned around. That went on for three days and three nights. At last, after much difficulty, they wakened Al Rhoole. He found the hair under his head, but no sign of Al Giseima. He smelled her scent and the scent of another human in his room. The *mufraka* and the Mungar told him what had happened. Al Rhoole began to run after the couple.

⋆⇒◉⇐⋆

Afraid of being followed, Wad Annameer asked Al Giseima, "Look back! Do you see anything?"

She answered, "No, I see nothing."

They rode even faster, and Al Rhoole chased, running after them. Three days passed. Then Wad Annameer asked, "Do you see anything?"

Al Giseima said she could now see Al Rhoole carrying his *mufraka* and the Mungar, but they were all as small as a fly. After another whole day of riding and being chased, Al Giseima said they were as large as a cock.

Still, Al Rhoole chased them. Two days later Al Rhoole and his *mufraka* and the Mungar were as big as a sheep. Day after day he chased them. Day after day Al Rhoole gained and the distance between them lessened. Al Rhoole seemed larger and larger. He became as big as a donkey.... as big as a horse... as big as a camel.... as big as an elephant. Now he was as big as a cloud.

It was at this point that Wad Annameer threw the *hijleej* thorn. A very thick thorny forest grew between the couple and their pursuer, and they ran faster and faster for their lives. Asked what she saw then, Al Giseima answered that she saw the thickest forest she had ever seen in her life. Two days later, being pursued by Al Rhoole and his things, Wad Annameer asked Al Giseima if she saw anything then. Al Rhoole and his things were once again as small as a fly. Then the same thing began to happen. Two days later Al Rhoole looked the size of a cock... a sheep... a donkey... a camel... an elephant... as large as the clouds in the sky.

It was then time for Wad Annameer to throw the stone. A great mountain appeared instantly. That gave them another good chance to avoid being caught by Al Rhoole. They ran for three days, before Al Giseima looked back to see Al Rhoole the size of a fly. Every time they ran, Al Rhoole gained and the distance between them lessened.

When Al Rhoole was again as large as the clouds, Wad Annameer threw the mud. A large lake appeared between them. Al Rhoole began to drink and drink and drink. His stomach got bigger and bigger and bigger. He was the size of a mountain.

Then there was a thundering explosion. Al Rhoole's stomach had burst, because the water he drank was too much for him. He died.

Al Giseima, in Wad Annameer's company, arrived safely at the village. There were the best ceremonies of marriage that had ever been held. Even the great-great-grandfather hadn't seen such ceremonies in all his life.

The lamps were lit. All the girls danced. Each girl's face was even brighter than all the lamps put together, brighter than the moon itself.

When the bride came to dance, she was like daylight, as bright as the sun itself. She forgave the six girls.

Wad Annameer and Al Giseima had many sons and daughters. The daughters were as beautiful as their mother, and the sons were as brave as their father.

⊷═◎═⊷

"Their great-great-grandson is the chief of your village, the Sheikh of our village," Omer told the children gathered around him.

They all cried, "Oh, is great-grandfather, Sheikh Ibrahim, your friend, her descendant?"

"Yes, and I am too, we are cousins. All of you here, sitting around me, are her descendants."

All the boys and girls were pleased and cried for joy. Dawn was creeping upon the earth. The white eagle of dawn had beaten the crow of night. They went to their homes to sleep, but Sheikh Omer, at that old age, saddled his donkey and went to his plantation after having his breakfast at that early hour.

THE CLEVER
SHEIKH OF THE BUTANA

Many tents were scattered over a wide area of the Butana, that piece of land that lies east of the river known as the Blue Nile in the Sudan. The tents marked the capital of Sheikh Hamad, who was the ruler of the tribes that lived in the Butana.

One day Sheikh Hamad received a visitor, who was on his way to a far-off town. The traveler was hosted very generously by Sheikh Hamad, as is the custom of the Sudanese. The Sheikh slew a big ox for the visitor and asked all the people to come for supper with the traveler. They had their supper and after that they sat listening to songs of bravery and stories of how they defeated their opponents from other tribes. They listened to music played on a flute called a *zumbara*, and every tune, or *loda*, told of a certain event.

At last, in the middle of the night, the feast came to an end and the guest was taken to his tent to sleep.

In the morning, unfortunately, the guest found that his money was gone, all of it. It hadp been stolen. A thief had broken into the tent while the people of the tribe were honoring the guest and making the feast for him.

The guest told Sheikh Hamad about the theft. Sheikh Hamad said to him, "Don't tell anybody about this. In the evening, when all the people come to the feast, we shall get your money back."

The day passed very slowly, and the guest spent the long hours thinking about his lost money, if it was going to be returned to him, and how.

In the evening, another ox was slain for the guest and the people of the tribe. The Sheikh's four wives, the women of the tribe, and the servants cooked the food. All the people were invited and all of them came.

After they had eaten, enjoyed themselves, listened to many songs and *zumbara lodas*, Sheikh Hamad stood up and addressed the people. "Well, our guest has lost all his money. Whoever took it or found it lying on the ground, let him step forward now and give it back." Nobody came forward.

Then the Sheikh said to them, "My donkey is in that tent. I want every man here to enter the tent, take hold of the donkey's tail, then come out the other entrance. Make sure you hold the tail of the donkey. If the one who holds the tail is innocent, nothing will happen to him, but when the one who has taken the money holds the tail, the donkey will bray. So go."

The first man entered and came out by the other door. Nothing happened. The second did the same. Nothing happened. The third, the fourth. But still nothing happened. Every man entered and came out, but the donkey didn't make any sound.

The Sheikh then asked the men to stand in a row and he went from one to the next. He took each man's hands, put them near his face, and then let them go. One by one he did this. Then the Sheikh took the hands of one of the men, put them near his face, very near his nose, and ordered him to step out.

He said to the man, "You have stolen the money. I want it brought now." The man tried his best to deny it, but Sheikh Hamad told him that the more he denied it, the worse his punishment would be. The Sheikh whispered in the thief's ear, "I oiled my donkey's tail with scented *dihn* oil. All the innocent people took hold of it and the scent of the *dihn* was in their palms, but, because you were afraid that the donkey might bray, you didn't hold it. And the *dihn* scent didn't get on your hands. Bring the money now, or you will curse the day on which your mother gave birth to you."

The man, accompanied by two of the Sheikh's guards, went away, dug a hole in the ground, and brought the money. The man promised not to do such a thing ever again. He was forgiven and was given part of the money to begin a new, honest life.

DIREIB ASSO

Once in the far distant past, when everyone spoke the same language, when everyone understood everything, there lived a brother and a sister.

The brother's name was Jabir. His sister's name was Direib Asso. They loved each other very much.

Jabir used to go to the forest early in the day. He went there to hunt rabbits, and to milk gazelles and antelopes. He brought the meat and the milk to his sister.

Every day he walked the distance between his house and the forest, on the bank of the Nile.

When he came home he would sing a song to his sister to open the door for him:

> Direib Asso,
> Your brother has come,
> Open the door.

It goes like this in Sudanese Arabic:

> *Direib Asso,*
> *Akhayik jo,*
> *Aftaheelul bab.*

She always answered him,

Welcome, welcome,
You who have come,
You bring dinner,
You bring supper,
To your sister.

Which, in Sudanese Arabic, is like this:

Marhab beik,
Ya tarhadi,
Ya ta'ashi,
Utjeeb labana seid,
Lekhaytak di.

She opened the door, they ate, drank the milk, then she oiled his skin to help him relax, and they both slept until morning.

Every day, early in the morning, Jabir walked to the forest. Before going, he always reminded his sister about their violently hostile and aggressive enemy, the wolf. He always said to her, "The wolf will come to you and try to open the door or deceive you into opening it for him. Never open the door for him."

One evening as the wolf was going by he heard Jabir singing to his sister.

Direib Asso,
Your brother has come,
Open the door.

He heard her reply. He thought of a plan to trick Direib Asso into opening the door so he could eat her.

The next morning, when Jabir went to the forest, the wolf came to the door. He began to sing in the ugliest voice imaginable:

Direib Asso
Akhayik jo
Aftaheelul bab.

24

She knew that that ugly voice was the wolf's voice, not her brother's voice. She answered him:

Your voice is like a donkey's voice,
And my brother's voice is like a ringing bell.

It is like this in Sudanese Arabic:

Hissak hiss humar,
U hiss Jabir akhuy jarasan tallal.

Then the wolf went away. He continued to think about a way he could make Direib Asso open the door for him.

He went to the blacksmith and said, "Oh, blacksmith, I want you to make something so my voice will sound like a ringing bell, or else I'll eat you."

The blacksmith was very frightened. He took his instruments and began working very hard on the wolf's mouth, tongue, teeth, and throat. After some time he was satisfied and stopped working.

He said to the wolf, "Now look here, wolf, I have done a very good job in your mouth. Your voice, now, is just like a ringing bell. But whatever you do, don't eat a dead body, and if you come across an ant nest, don't roll on it."

The wolf went away. On his way, he came across a dead goat. It was a fat goat. He was hungry. He dashed to the dead goat and devoured it, leaving only the bones.

He continued on his way to Direib Asso. Then his skin began to itch him. He saw an ant nest. He was very pleased, and began to roll on it.

By early evening, before Jabir arrived home to his sister, the wolf was there. He began to sing:

Direib Asso,
Akhayik jo, (Your brother has come)
Aftahilul bab. (Open the door)

His voice was even worse than before. She knew he was the wolf. She answered:

Hissak hiss humar, (Your voice is like a donkey's)
Hiss Jabir akhuy (The voice of my brother, Jabir)
Jarasan tallal. (Is a ringing bell.)

The wolf got very angry when he did not succeed in eating

Direib Asso. He went away frustrated.

When Jabir came, Direib Asso told him that the wolf had tried twice to deceive her. But, she told Jabir, his voice was very ugly and rough.

This made Jabir uneasy. Before going to the forest the next day, he said to her, "Direib Asso, I didn't sleep well last night. I thought all the time about the wolf. I am afraid something bad may happen to you. Be careful! Don't open the door to anybody until I come back!"

Meanwhile, the wolf went to the blacksmith again and said to him, "Oh blacksmith, if you don't make my voice sound like a ringing bell, I shall eat you."

The blacksmith was very frightened, and began his work again on the wolf's tongue, teeth, and throat.

After he finished the job, he said to the wolf, "I warn you for the second time: Don't eat dead bodies, and don't roll on ant nests."

The wolf went on his way to Direib Asso. A fat sheep was lying dead by the road. He was hungry. He hadn't eaten since the previous day. He felt he must have a meal now.

When he was about to eat, he remembered that he should not. So he went on without eating, although his saliva ran like a river.

He came across an ant nest, and his skin began to itch him. He was going to roll on it, but again he remembered the blacksmith's warning. He went away without rolling on it.

Before Jabir arrived at his house, the wolf was there. He stood at the door, cleared his throat, and began to sing. Now his voice was as beautiful as a ringing bell. Mistaking him for her brother Jabir, Direib Asso opened the door.

She was horrified. Standing in front of her was a huge ugly wolf with an open mouth full of very sharp teeth.

Without giving Direib Asso a second to think, the wolf dashed in and closed the door behind him. He opened his wide, mean, horrible mouth.

Direib Asso had to think quickly. She was sure that if she could delay the wolf a little, her brother would come, kill the wolf, and save her.

The wolf said to her, "I am going to kill you and eat you."

Direib Asso said to him, "If you want to eat just bones, I'll be a good meal for you. But if you want fat, fleshy meat, you better wait for Jabir.

He will be a good meal for you." She knew that Jabir and his three dogs would kill the wolf.

The wolf imagined a good fat meal, and agreed to wait.

Jabir came and sang to his sister to open the door. The door was opened, but by a fearful, ugly, and huge wolf, who pulled Jabir inside the house and snatched away his spear.

The wolf said, "I am now going to kill you and have a good meal of your fleshy meat."

Jabir said to the wolf, "You know human flesh is best after a song. Let me sing a song! You will hear a good song and will have a nice meal."

The wolf said, "I am not in a hurry. Take your time! Sing your song!"

Jabir began his song, calling for his three hunting dogs. The song went like this:

> Bureiba, Bureiba,
> Admiringly swift,
> Masaga'a, Masaga'a
> As swift as lightning,
> Fulla, Fulla,
> As swift as a bullet,
> Your master is about to be killed.

It sounds like this in Sudanese Arabic:

> *Bureiba, Bureiba,*
> *Wassura'a ajeeba,*
> *Masaga'a Masaga'a*
> *Ya hajar assaga'a,*
> *Fulla, ya fulla,*
> *Sare'etan julla,*
> *Seedkan magtul.*

Three fearful, huge, and strong dogs suddenly appeared. Jabir ordered the three dogs to attack and kill the wolf. A fearful fight took place, but the dogs were victorious and the wolf was soon killed.

Jabir told his dogs to eat the wolf and only to leave his teeth and the muscles of the neck. He pulled out the teeth of the dead wolf and fixed them to a piece of wood.

The neck muscles were then stretched between the teeth. That was the best musical instrument ever made. Jabir played beautiful music with his instrument.

Direib Asso married a strong hunter.

Jabir married a beautiful wife.

They all had sons and daughters.

They lived long happy lives in that lovely house until death came upon them a long time later.

THE DJINNY BROTHER

When I was a small child my grandmother told me that a long time ago, in the far distant past, there lived three wicked brothers. Their names were Himhim, Zimzim, and Timtim.

Their father was dead, and they lived with their poor unhappy mother.

They were not at all good to her. They were all very cruel to her. They did not help her in any way. They just demanded food, water, and clothing. Himhim and Zimzim were the worst sons ever born to a woman. Timtim was a bit better than his two brothers, but still he was very bad. Their mother tried her best to bring them up as good people, but she failed. She simply couldn't do so, by any means.

One day, when she felt hopeless about her sons, she left her house and went into the wilderness, in the worst heat of the day, in the hottest month of the summer.

The summer, there near the equator, was and still is unbearable. The heat reaches over one hundred and twenty degrees most days.

She walked and she walked.

The heat was severe and the sun felt as if it was just overhead. It was like walking in an oven full of fire. She was about to be baked by the sun. She got very tired. Thirst was about to kill her.

Far away she saw a tree. It was a *hijleej* tree. Elves, leprechauns, and Rhooles always live under the roots of *hijleej* trees. (If you have never met Al Rhoole, you would not want to. He is mean, and ugly, and always looking for ways to make trouble.)

31

She sat in the shade under the thick branches of that tree.

The tree was owned by Al Rhoole.

She found a clay jar full of clear cold water near her feet. She drank her fill of that water.

She did not know that both the jar and what it contained were magic.

Having drunk that water, she became pregnant. She felt she must go back home, because she was soon going to give birth.

No sooner had she gone home than she gave birth to a baby boy.

The seventh day after a birth is the day when people traditionally give names to their newborn children, boys and girls. They slay a sheep or two to celebrate.

His brothers brought a fat sheep to slay. Then something very strange happened. The baby, seven days old, began to speak.

"Oh! I came from my mother's stomach with a name. My name is Rimaydun. Don't slay the sheep! I want that sheep. Leave it for me! I am the son of the djinny Al Rhoole, the husband of Al Rhoola," said the infant. (People believe that a djinny is a spirit that can take on a human form, and have special powers over people.)

His mother and his brothers were astonished to hear a seven-day-old baby speak. They left the sheep for him.

Rimaydun grew up quickly and began to go with his brothers to the farm. The three brothers rode on their three donkeys and Rimaydun rode on his sheep. The sheep walked step by step with the three donkeys. The donkeys could never be in front of the sheep.

But when they reached the farm, the three brothers did nothing; they never worked. Rimaydun did all the work.

They lived happily, but still the three brothers were cruel to their mother.

One day Al Rhoola saw the boys. All Rhoolas are bad enemies of human beings, but that Rhoola was the most wicked, dangerous, and cruel one of all. She saw the boys and decided to eat them all. She hesitated, because they were always together and because there was that djinny brother, Rimaydun. She decided that she must eat them or cause them catastrophes by making them ill, blind, or deaf.

Coming back from their farm, the four came across a big, fat, beautiful donkey. Himhim, the eldest of the brothers, said, "I'll take this beautiful donkey, it will be mine." He went toward it.

Rimaydun said to him, "Don't do that, Himhim! This is Al Rhoola, who has changed herself into a donkey." Because Himhim was cruel to his mother and didn't obey anybody, he didn't pay any attention to what his brother had said to him. He caught the donkey and jumped on its back.

The donkey ran swifter than lightning. It jumped high in the air and threw Himhim to a far place called the Islands of Warh Al Warh, where many Rhooles, Rhoolas, and other evil spirits make their home. There he found Al Rhoola waiting for him. She swallowed him. She hid him in her stomach, so that he would never be found again.

Many days followed. Then Al Rhoola decided to swallow another one of the remaining two brothers. She changed herself into a horse. She waited for the brothers on the way between their house and their field.

Zimzim, now the eldest brother, decided to take the horse. He said, "Oh, what a strong horse! I'll have that horse. It will take the place of my lazy donkey."

Rimaydun said, "Zimzim, don't do that. This is Al Rhoola. Remember your lost brother. She will do to you what she has done to him."

But Zimzim refused to listen to his brother. He was also cruel to his mother. He went to the horse. He rode on her back. The horse ran until she reached her house. There she changed into Al Rhoola and swallowed Zimzim, hiding him in her stomach.

After some time, when Timtim and Rimaydun were going back home from their farm, they were met by a pretty maiden. Timtim said, "I want to marry this sweet girl."

His brother, Rimaydun, said to him, "Don't forget what happened to your elder brothers when they didn't listen to me. This is Al Rhoola. She will do to you as she has done to your brothers."

Timtim didn't pay attention to what his djinny brother said. He married the beautiful girl, who was really Al Rhoola. When Timtim went to his wife that night, Rimaydun was under their bed. Whenever Al Rhoola tried to deafen or blind Timtim, Rimaydun was in the way.

Al Rhoola said to Timtim, "Your brother Rimaydun is under the bed."

When Timtim looked under the bed to see his brother, Rimaydun was outside.

Al Rhoola quickly closed the door, pulled out Timtim's eyes, and in a second she was flying to her country. She left Timtim crying in pain.

Because Timtim was not completely cruel to his mother, only a little cruel, he lived, but he lived blind. Rimaydun said to Timtim that he would do all that he could to bring him back his eyes.

In the course of time Rimaydun's sheep grew and grew. It became larger than the donkey, but smaller than the horse. Its tail grew very long and very strong.

Rimaydun, on the back of his sheep, traveled from place to place. He began a long journey, asking all the witches he met how to return his brother's eyes to him. He visited many healers, too.

A healer told him that he should take a big gourd and a large quantity of wool and go to where Al Rhoola lived. He should deceive her and try to take his brother's eyes from her.

Hearing that, Rimaydun rode his sheep, took a gourd that he put under his clothes, on his stomach, and put the wool on his head. He looked like a pregnant girl.

He went to Al Rhoola's house, pretending that he was her pregnant niece, and said to her, "O Auntie! I am your dead sister's daughter. I am pregnant. I am going to give birth soon. My mother, before she died, told me to come to you when I am ready to deliver my baby. When I give birth, please kill this sheep for the naming of the baby."

Al Rhoola accepted Rimaydun, believing he was her niece. Then Rimaydun said, "I need to relieve myself." Al Rhoola showed him where to go. Rimaydun went there and mixed some of the wool with his urine to look like the urine of a Rhoola, which is always mixed with wool. Al Rhoola, finding the urine full of wool, was satisfied that Rimaydun was her niece.

Rimaydun said to Al Rhoola, "My other sister, who is married to a merchant in a far away city, is blind. How can I cure her?" Al Rhoola, very eager to help, answered, "I have got two eyes of a boy called Timtim.

I'll give them to you to cure your sister. I don't want to keep them with me any longer. Take them, cure your sister, and come back to me soon, because I think that you are going to have your baby very soon. Don't delay in coming back!"

Rimaydun took the two eyes, got on the back of his sheep, and rode away. Al Rhoola asked him, "Why are you running away, as if you are stealing a thing, niece?"

Rimaydun answered her, "I'm not your niece, I'm Rimaydun, and I am in a hurry to cure my brother, Timtim, with his own eyes, which you had taken away."

Al Rhoola flew in the air trying to catch him and kill him. His sheep's tail became a long sharp sword, struck Al Rhoola in her stomach, opened it, and out came Himhim, fat and strong. Rimaydun helped him up onto the sheep's back.

Al Rhoola changed her stomach into another one and attacked severely. She was about to get hold of Rimaydun when the tail changed into a sharp butcher's knife, opened her stomach, and Zimzim came out. He was no less healthy than his brother. Zimzim was put on the sheep's back, near his two brothers.

Al Rhoola changed her stomach for the third time. She flew swiftly in the air. Her teeth were now as long and sharp as knives. She dove at the brothers from among the clouds. Rimaydun threw the wool and gourd in her direction. The gourd broke into thousands of pieces and penetrated her body. The wool went into her nose, her eyes, her ears, her mouth, and every wound in her body made by the broken pieces of the gourd.

She became deaf, dumb, and blind, and couldn't breathe. A rain of blood came from all parts of her body. She fell dead.

The three brothers, with their sheep, reached home safely. Timtim's eyes were put back and he could see as before. They asked their mother to pardon them. She did so with the love of all mothers. She blessed them. Together they all lived a long, happy life full of love.

THE DONKEY, THE WOLF, AND THE FOX

I t is told that a donkey lived in the old times, long, long ago, when everything talked the same language. The donkey was very hungry all summer long. Of course, summer in the Sudan is severely hot and full of hot winds and sand. There is no spring. After summer comes the rainy season, called *al Kharief* (the autumn, between July and the middle of October).

The donkey was very hungry all summer long. He was very thin. He became just skin and bones. He was about to die.

And then, when the rain came, the grass grew very green and healthy. All the grass was full of flowers, and stretched as far as the horizon, as far as the eye could see.

The donkey went out of his house, out of the village. He went to the countryside, near the forest, and began to eat the best food, the best grass.

He went on eating and eating, enjoying every bite he ate, enjoying himself, enjoying every minute of his time there. For days he didn't go back to the village. He was now fat and strong.

One day, suddenly, he heard in the grass a whisper of feet moving stealthily behind him. Slowly he turned his head to look back. He saw an ugly wolf creeping toward him with an open mouth full of sharp white teeth.

The wolf was crawling slowly, slowly, step by step, until he was only a spear's throw from the donkey. The wolf was trying to catch the donkey, to kill him and eat him.

Seeing the wolf so very near, the donkey ran at full speed. The wolf pursued him. The donkey ran fast, but the wolf was at his tail. The donkey ran faster, but the wolf followed, determined to catch him and make a good meal out of his fat body.

The donkey ran faster and faster, as fast as he could, but the wolf still followed swiftly, and was just at the donkey's tail.

When the donkey saw that there was no hope of getting rid of the wolf, he turned and ran onto a piece of land that was very muddy and swampy. He ran no more than ten or fifteen yards, then got stuck in the mud.

The wolf, discovering that the donkey could not go further because he was stuck, and being so very hungry, followed the donkey into the mud. He ran about ten yards, but less than five paces from the donkey he got stuck also.

The wolf was very near the donkey, but could not reach him. He tried harder and harder, because his hunger compelled him. The more he tried, the more the mud caught him. Now his whole chest and most of his neck were in the mud. In vain he tried to reach the donkey.

Losing hope, he thought it was better to go back. To his amazement, he couldn't. He was stuck between the road and the donkey. He couldn't move either way. He was very tired from trying. He was caught between the devil and the deep blue sea.

And then Abul Hussein, the fox, came walking along the road. Abul Hussein is known for his cleverness, his wisdom, and most times, his wickedness. He has many tricks. He tricks the hens in the village, tricks their owners, tricks the fishermen, tricks all the different animals and even tricks the majestic king, the lion. He is very clever in getting free of traps and difficult places, and sometimes helps other animals when they are trapped or find themselves in a difficult spot.

The wolf cried to him, "O Abul Hussein, I am in a very critical situation."

Abul Hussein was, at that moment, in a mood of utmost wickedness and deceit. So he asked the wolf, "What is this critical situation you find yourself in?"

"I tried to reach my meal, the donkey, and couldn't. I tried to get back and it was impossible."

The fox said, "The critical position and the worst of your time hasn't come yet."

The wolf now found himself very miserable, because of the words of the fox, and he said, "When is this worst time coming?"

Abul Hussein answered, "That time will come when the sun rises and the mud dries and catches your four legs; when the donkey's master discovers the donkey's absence and looks for him; when the master traces the tracks of his donkey and at last finds you in this position. Of course the donkey's master will be carrying his gun." The wolf began to howl. He howled until he died of fear.

When the sun came up, the master began to look for his donkey. He looked in the house, in the street, out of the village, in the countryside. There, he found his donkey in the mud, and near him a dead wolf. He skinned the wolf and made a good coat of his skin.

FATMA THE RED STRAW

Once upon a time, when everything spoke the same language, when all things understood all things, there was a village of very happy people on the river known as the Blue Nile in the Sudan.

The people were generous and good to each other.

The elder people cared for the younger boys and girls and made them happy. The younger boys and girls obeyed all the older people of the village. All the older people felt themselves to be like parents to every young boy or girl in the village.

All the girls were beautiful and all the boys were smart, strong, and generous.

One of the most beautiful girls was Fatma the Red Straw.

She was called the Red Straw, because in the Sudan, there is the very sweet and beautiful straw of the sugar cane. Calling her the Red Straw meant that she was beautiful.

She had very long black hair, wide black eyes, and a straight nose. Her face was round like the moon, and her color was like ripe wheat.

She had a very smart brother, who was also generous, courageous, and strong. His name was Dukhry.

He had a lovely strong horse. One day he took his horse to the Nile to drink. While she was drinking, something stuck in her throat and she began to choke. Dukhry took his horse to the *baseer*, the healer, who found a very long hair in the horse's throat. Dukhry thought that that hair could have killed his horse. He decided to marry the girl to whom the hair belonged, if ever he could find her.

He went to an old woman in the village and asked her to try to find the girl whose hair his horse had swallowed. He promised to give the old woman a fine gift, if she could find the girl.

Taking the hair in her hand, the old woman went to each girl in the village and held the hair up to her head to see if it matched.

One by one, from house to house, from street to street, from lane to lane, she searched to find the girl whose hair matched that single hair.

At last she found that the hair belonged to Fatma the Red Straw, who was the sister of Dukhry himself, the owner of the horse. He insisted on marrying the girl whose hair had almost killed his horse.

Now Fatma did not accept that. She spoke to her six girlfriends. "Now look here girls! If Dukhry marries me, a custom will be started that every man who has a beautiful sister will be able to marry her. This is against all the laws that human beings have known."

They decided that they must flee. They must leave their village forever. They must run away.

Taking some food and some water and a bundle of clothes, the girls went out of the village in the dead of night. They began their flight to the unknown.

They went a long way until they reached a forest. They went deep in the forest until they came to a huge cave.

In that cave lived an old Rhoole, a very fearful sort of being that liked to eat flesh, especially the flesh of people, and most especially the flesh of young girls.

Because he was very old, he could not find food easily. Sometimes he went hungry for days. So he decided to keep the girls with him. Then, when a chance came, he would kill one of them, cook her, hide her flesh, and eat her day after day after day.

He would first eat the girl who was the fattest, then the second, the third, the fourth, the fifth, the sixth, and at last the seventh.

But before he ate them he wanted to make them fat. He mixed up special foods to fatten the girls.

He was so happy about his good fortune that he talked to himself about his plan. Fatma the Red Straw heard him talking to himself.

She did not tell any of the girls, but decided to save her friends and herself by killing Al Rhoole before he could kill them all.

While she waited for a chance, she became very helpful to Al Rhoole. Whenever he called for any of them to help him, Fatma the Red Straw hurried to him. He liked her very much. After some time the girls were fat enough.

Again Al Rhoole spoke to himself and Fatma the Red Straw heard him. She heard him say that that night, when the girls were asleep, he would take one of them, kill her, cook her, hide her flesh, and eat it day after day.

So Fatma the Red Straw said to him, "O father, will you tell me, if someone wants to take the skin of an old Rhoole, what would one do?"

He said to her, "Oh my girl, do you want to kill me and take my skin?"

She said to him, "No, father, I am asking about an old Rhoole and you are not. You have been generous to us, you have kept us in your house, you fed us, you gave us water, you gave us every protection, you gave us every good thing. How can I think of killing you?" He was very pleased, thinking that he had deceived the girls.

He said, "Well, you get a thorn of the *hijleej* tree and when he is asleep, put it in the middle of his head, and then with one stroke of a stone you hit the thorn and all his skin will come off. Remember to strike only once, no more than that."

When the girls went to collect wood for the fire, Fatma the Red Straw found a very large thorn of a *hijleej* tree. She hid it under her clothes, along with a heavy stone.

When Al Rhoole was fast asleep, Fatma the Red Straw began to walk toward him slowly, step by step, until she was standing by his head.

Quickly she took out the thorn, put it near the middle of his head, and struck one strong blow with the stone. The thorn went deep into his head, and all the skin came off the body of the old Rhoole. He was dead.

The girls went on living in the cave. They were very happy there.

Time passed, and one day, when they were in the forest collecting food and firewood, a group of horsemen rode into the forest.

The girls saw the men and fled to their cave.

The men also saw the girls, and they dashed after them on their horses.

Fatma the Red Straw quickly put on the skin of the old Rhoole. She now looked like a very old man with wrinkled skin.

When the first man entered the cave, he saw six beautiful girls with an old man. He chose the most beautiful girl and brought her out. When they were outside the birds in the forest began to sing.

> He took the leaf from those,
> He left the prettiest rose.

In Arabic, the song goes like this:

> *Shal aluwar,*
> *Khalla alnuwar.*

The men were all astonished, because the girl seemed to be very beautiful. But the man who brought that girl out was the most astonished, because he knew that he had chosen the most beautiful of the six girls.

The second man entered the cave and brought out the most beautiful girl of the five remaining girls. Again the birds on the top of the trees sang the same song:

> He took the leaf from those,
> He left the prettiest rose.

> *Shal aluwar,*
> *Khalla alnuwar.*

Of course he was very astonished, because he knew that he had taken the prettiest of the five girls.

A third man entered and came out of the cave with the one he considered to be the most beautiful of the four remaining girls.

Yet again, the birds sang the same song from the treetops.

Another man entered, chose a girl, came out very happy,

but heard the song being sung for the fourth time.

Each man took one of the girls, brought her out and heard the same song being sung to him, telling him that he had chosen the leaf and left the rose.

At last there was only one young man left. He was the richest one among them, the strongest, the most handsome, and the smartest. His name was Badr.

Badr entered the cave to find that the only human being left for him was an old wrinkled man. He did not know that the old man was really Fatma the Red Straw, the prettiest of all the girls.

Badr said, "I can take you to live with me, grandfather, although I would have liked to have one of the girls whom I could have married. You can be a shepherd for my animals." But when he took the old man out, all the birds in the forest began to sing:

> He was the one who chose,
> He took the prettiest rose.

> *Shal alnuwar,*
> *Khalla aluwar.*

His friends began to laugh at the song of the birds, and at what Badr had found: an old wrinkled man, who could be of no use despite the singing of the birds.

They all went to the village.

The next day Badr said to the old man, "Oh, grandfather,"—for the Sudanese usually call the old men grandfathers, fathers or uncles, even if they are of no relation to each other—"what shall I give you to look after? Shall I give you my camels, so you can look after them?"

The old man said to him, "No, my son, the camels will bite me with their teeth."

He said to the old man, "Shall I give you the horses then?"

The old man said, "No, they will kick me with their hooves."

"Shall I give you the cows?"

"I can't do that, they have got long horns and they will kill me."

"Shall I give you the goats and sheep?"

"No, they will hit me with their heads."

"Shall I give you the geese and the swans?"

Now the old man said, "Yes, I like geese. I like swans. I will take them to the river, they will swim, and then I will bring them back."

So the old man was given the geese and the swans to care for. He took them down to the Nile. They made happy sounds, "Quack, quack, quack, quack."

Badr sent one of his servants with the old man, who was really Fatma the Red Straw.

The servant was deaf and mute: he couldn't hear, and he couldn't speak. As the sun was about to set, Fatma the Red Straw took off the skin of the old man and she put her jewels and gold on a rock. She entered the Blue Nile and she began to bathe and swim in the water.

When the servant saw her he could not believe how beautiful she was. His eyes opened as big as cups. His jaw dropped. His mouth opened in astonishment.

Then Fatma put her jewelry back on, along with the old man's skin, and went back to the village.

When the servant went to his master, he tried to speak. "Ab bah ba, a ba." He put his hand on his neck to tell his master about her jewels. He put his hands on his breasts, to tell his master how very beautiful she was. He put his hand up, aiming at the moon to say she was as beautiful as the moon.

Then the master, Badr, said to Fatma the Red Straw, "What is this servant trying to say?"

"He is saying to you that he will tell Allah that you treated him badly and Allah will slay you. That is why he is pointing to his neck, and he will hit you in the chest."

This made Badr angry, and he killed the servant.

The next day he sent another deaf, dumb servant with Fatma the Red Straw, and the same thing happened again.

The servant tried to tell his master how beautiful that girl was, how she looked like the moon.

And Badr said, "Oh, grandfather, what does he say?"

Fatma the Red Straw said, "I think there is something that aches him in his neck and in his chest. You must bring the *baseer*."

The *baseer* came with very long pieces of lead. He put the lead in the fire, so as to cure the servant, but when he put the lead on his neck and on his chest, the servant died.

The same thing happened again with a third deaf mute servant.

On the fourth day another deaf and mute servant was sent. But this time Badr went ahead of them, and hid near a rock in thick bushes on the bank of the Nile.

In the late afternoon, Fatma the Red Straw took off the skin of the old man. She appeared as beautiful as the moon. She put her gold and jewelry on the rock and then went into the water. When she came out she put on the old man's skin again.

Badr ran back to his house after seeing this. Now he knew the exact meaning of the song of the birds.

When the old man and the servant returned, the servant tried to tell his master that this was not an old man at all, but a very beautiful girl, who had a lot of gold and jewels.

Again Fatma made up a story so the master would not know what the servant was really trying to say.

Then the master said to Fatma the Red Straw, "Do you know how to play *sieja?*" This is a game of strategy, played by two people. Each tries to capture the other's playing pieces, which are stones of different colors.

She said, "Yes, I can play."

He said, "Let us play a game. If I win I will skin you and if you win you will skin me."

Fatma the Red Straw was very clever at *sieja*, so she agreed. She said to him, "Oh, my son, it's all right with me. Let us play."

The master got a very sharp knife and put it between them, and they began to play *sieja*.

After some time Fatma won the first game, and the master said, "Now grandfather, skin me."

And Fatma said to him, "No, I will spare you this time."

They played another game and again the old man won.

Badr said, "Grandfather, now do it."

Fatma replied, "No, I'll spare you this time also."

They played seven games, and every time the old man won. Yet each time he did not take the skin of the master.

On the eighth round the master won, and he said, "Now my grandfather, I must skin you."

The old man said to him, "But, my son, I spared you seven times, won't you spare me this one time?"

The master said, "No, it was up to you to skin me and you refused. I will not refuse. I must skin you."

He caught the skin of the old man with the sharp knife, and all the skin fell off. There appeared the most beautiful girl, Fatma the Red Straw.

Badr asked her name. She told him. Then he asked her if she would marry him.

They married, and had many sons.

All of them were strong, brave, and generous.

They had many daughters, each as beautiful as Fatma herself.

They went on living until death came upon them many, many years later.

THE FOX LEARNS
HOW TO DIVIDE

O nce in a very thick forest full of fierce animals, green trees, running streams, and all things that animals need to make them happy, there lived a lion. He was king of that forest. The wolf and the fox, known as Abul Hussein, were the lion's friends and were the most senior ministers of the kingdom. They were close to one another and to the king, the lion. Wherever the lion was, it was sure they would be found.

They walked together, slept together, and did everything else together. The wolf and Abul Hussein shared bits of wisdom with the king. The kingdom under the rule of the three animals was at its peak.

When the lion ate any of the animals of the forest, both the wolf and Abul Hussein ate after him. Sometimes when the animal was big enough, they were allowed to eat at the same time as his majesty.

Whenever the lion ate one of the animals, the other animals became uneasy and were afraid of being eaten. They moved to the edge of the forest, leaving the three friends to themselves.

Once, not finding enough food for days after the flight of the animals, the lion, the wolf, and Abul Hussein began to feel hungry. Day after day they looked for a feast, but in vain. Not a single animal was to be found. Life became very difficult.

Then one day, while they were walking wearily around the forest, the lion thought he saw three different things. He asked his ministers what they saw. The wolf thought he saw the trunk of a tree and two branches. Abul Hussein moved cautiously toward the things, hiding himself among some bushes. After some time he came back with the best news.

He told them that those things were a sleeping zebra, an antelope, and a rabbit. All three were fast asleep. The king, for some time, couldn't move for pleasure. Finally, he ordered the two ministers not to make a sound and to wait there until he called them.

Stealthily he moved, very slowly and cautiously, until he reached the sleeping animals. Hunger gave him a strength that he had never had before or ever dreamed of having. With one stroke the zebra was dead, and each paw of the lion held one of the other two animals. The rabbit soon died, and the antelope was then caught by the king's teeth on his throat. He kicked his legs for a short time, but he soon suffocated and died.

The lion called for his ministers, who came, very glad and pleased. Each spoke to himself about the fresh lovely meal that would satisfy him. Each knew that the lion would eat the zebra, the wolf would have the antelope, and the rabbit would be Abul Hussein's meal.

They reached the spot. The ministers sat behind the king, waiting to obtain his permission to begin the feast. They waited and waited; the king seemed to have forgotten all the hunger of the past days, the long days they had spent without meals.

At last the king ordered the wolf to come into his presence. The wolf moved quickly, with happy anticipation. Then the king asked, "How would you divide these animals?"

The wolf already knew the division. He said, "The zebra is for his majesty, the king, because it is the biggest meal. Abul Hussein, being the smallest, will take the rabbit which is enough for him and will satisfy his hunger. The antelope will be my share of the meal." Then he gave a broad smile, enjoying his wisdom.

The king raised his left front leg and brought it down on the wolf's neck. The wolf's head flew away and his body twitched this way and that until he died.

Now the king asked Abul Hussein to come into his presence. Abul Hussein came, with wide eyes and shaking legs. "Divide these animals!" ordered the king.

Abul Hussein answered, "The zebra is for the king's breakfast, the antelope is for the king's lunch, and the rabbit is for the king's supper."

The lion laughed and asked the fox, "Who taught you this wise way of dividing things? When did you learn this wisdom?"

Abul Hussein answered, "The head of the wolf, cut away from his body, taught me both this wisdom and this way of dividing things."

GENEROSITY
BENDS THE ROAD

Attay was a simple, courageous, and generous man who lived in the first quarter of the eighteenth century, in a small village. The village sat in a bend of the river far away from the caravan road. The small village was entirely populated by Attay's family. There were his wife, his seven sons, their wives, his nine daughters, their husbands, and about sixty-three of his grandchildren and great-grandchildren. Even some of these grand- and great-grandchildren had wives and children of their own. Their village was always expanding, because of the many offspring of the family.

Most people were farmers at that time. Even people who had different jobs—like carpentry, building, shoemaking, or any other jobs—were also farmers. The people of the Sudan in that village or any other place were really "jacks of all trades." The people of that village and most other villages did not need to travel or leave their villages for any reason, because all of them were farmers and there was more than enough land for tens of thousands to plant.

Life was prosperous. People thrived, and they did not need to emigrate to another village or town or city to live. Their only movement was to the big city to sell some of their animals and buy their household needs: dates, sugar, clothes, and other things of that sort.

In most cases in the Sudan young men marry their young cousins. If a young man from another village or another tribe wanted to marry one of the girls, the girl's father would ask him for some time to ask her relatives and make sure that her cousins would accept the marriage.

If one of the cousins wanted to marry the girl, she would marry her cousin. That was accepted by people and was considered a sign of virtue and moral excellence.

In that way the village grew and expanded. The caravan road was at a very great distance. The road itself crossed a very thick forest that extended for miles in all directions. One day a dozen merchants who were traveling in a caravan lost their way in that thick forest. Many days passed as they wandered in the forest, not knowing where to go.

One night, just before dawn, they were awakened by the crowing of many cocks for the dawn prayer. They also heard many dogs barking. Both the crowing of the cocks and the barking of the dogs came from far away, from a very great distance. Saddling their camels, they began moving toward what they had heard. At sunrise they saw a village about three miles away. They moved toward it. When they approached it, they saw many young men coming out of their houses and collecting outside the village, waiting for them with smiling faces and outstretched hands, welcoming them.

The merchants were greeted warmly and were taken to a wide yard, around which were many rooms. Their camels were unsaddled, tied, and were given grass, grain, and water.

The merchants saw an elderly man with twelve young men, each of whom was holding a sheep and a sharp knife. Each one of the young men threw down the sheep he was holding and slew it.

Each one of the twelve merchants was asked to jump over his "*karama* sheep." The *karama* is an animal slain for a guest or for Allah to feed the poor people who cannot pay for their meal. If one was ill and became well, one would slay an animal to feed the people as a way of thanking Allah.

When a woman gives birth to a baby, two sheep will be her *karama*, given at the naming of the baby, usually on the seventh day after a baby's birth, but sometimes on the fourteenth or the twenty-first day.

Sometimes grain is cooked in place of the animal as *karama*.

All these and other things done to thank Allah are called *karamas*. People thank Allah for bringing them a guest, making them well, or giving them children. There are different happenings and occasions for *karamas*. If a dear one comes after a long absence, a *karama* will be made for the return. All the people of the village will be asked to attend the meal. They will enjoy their time eating and hearing many songs praising and glorifying Allah and the Prophet.

So the lost merchants were hosted generously by Attay, whose name means "giver." The village people treated them well, and made them feel as if they belonged there. That went on for several days, until the merchants had rested well and were ready to continue their journey. They thanked Attay. Attay asked them to visit him again, and also asked them to bring other friends the next time. The merchants tried to give Attay many presents, which he refused. Finally, they set out on the road again.

Whenever the merchants went to a village or a town they told about Attay, his generosity, his sons, and the village. People began to tell others of that man, his sons, his grandsons, and the way they welcomed people. Soon afterwards, a party of the original group of "lost" merchants asked some other merchants who happened to be traveling with them in a caravan to leave the road and pay a visit to Attay. They accepted. Attay was very pleased to receive his old friends and even more pleased to be introduced to new friends. He hosted them very generously, as was his custom. After spending quite a few days with Attay, the new and the old friends continued on their journey. They spoke of their journey and their visit to Attay wherever they went and to whomever they met.

Now people who heard of Attay and his generosity, and were going by that road, visited Attay in his village. His fame spread all over the country as quickly and surely as fire in dry grass.

Year after year travelers visited Attay, either by chance, when they lost their way and found themselves near his village, or intentionally.

A time came when all caravans and travelers left the road and went to Attay's village, and it became the most important station on the road. When they went there, they were hosted in the best manner. They were given their food, the rooms where they slept, and anything else they needed. For all this, of course, they paid no money. In return, Attay would accept nothing. There are still people who live this way in the Sudan.

So it happened that, in the course of time, the straight road was diverted and bent to Attay's village. The road went straight no more. It turned to go to Attay's village, and then from the village it rejoined a further point on the road, about twenty miles from the first bend. The older straight road disappeared.

You will remember that Attay's name means "giver." Now, after the road of the caravans and travelers was diverted and bent to his village, he became known as Awaj Addarib, which means the one who diverted the straight road to one's village through his generosity. The word "*awaj*" means bent, and "*addarib*" means road. Awaj Addarib lived a long happy life. Even to this day, the people of that village are generous and loving to their guests. Every one of his descendants is called Wad Awaj Addarib, the son of the man who bent the road.

THE MAGIC RING

A learned, wise, religious man had one son. The man was devoted to Allah. He would do nothing against the Islamic teachings. His house was always open to all who were in need. By night he would walk through the streets of the town and throw money over the walls of the houses of the poor people who were in need but thought it humiliating to beg others for help. He helped everyone and never liked to be known. He did it only for Allah to know. He preached to people, telling them of the right way, the way that leads to heaven.

Everybody loved him. The man took good care of his only beloved son, whose name was Amin. He wanted his son to be better than himself. So the father had begun to teach Amin when he was very young.

By this time, Amin had finished his training. It was time to put what he had learned to practical tests, tests to show that what he had learned would not be in contradiction with the good and honest life.

Amin was very smart and good. He treated all elders with the deepest respect, and youngsters with sympathy, favor, and gentleness. Amin looked upon the young as a teacher does his students.

His father had business all over the country, with shops in many towns and cities. He wanted Amin to run the shops in a distant city. But one day he saw Amin with a group of bad young men. He was afraid that Amin's good manners would be changed and that what was once his good behavior would turn vulgar and offensive.

The father, knowing that Amin was moving from adolescence toward adulthood, thought he should tackle the matter very carefully.

That evening, he asked Amin to meet with him. He wanted to discuss some important matters and get his son's opinion on those and other matters.

When they were alone, they talked about their trade, its prospects, and how to use their profits wisely. Then the man said to his son, "Now Amin, let us, now and always, thank and love Allah for what he has given us, and what he always gives us. Let us try, all the time, to be with Him as He is always with us. But now let me give you what my father gave me when I began to work independently, freely, and in my own way. I feel that you must begin your own work and do most of the work yourself. I can still work, but I am not young and strong, as I used to be. Now I want you to look after me as I have always looked after you.

"I will give you now what my father gave me, when I began my work. Take this ring and put it on your finger. Whenever you are about to do wrong, the ring will prick you. In this way you will learn that what you are going to do is not right, and you will not do it. Of course, if you want to do right, the ring will not prick you."

So the son put on the ring and began his work.

One day a man came into the shop. He was interested in a certain piece of cloth. He said to Amin, "I will give you three times what you paid for it." Amin was very pleased. He had bought that piece of cloth for only one hundred pounds, and planned to sell it for one hundred and twenty pounds. He would now sell it for three hundred pounds.

"Money does not come that easily," he said to himself. "It is a matter of chance. If I say that its price is two thousand pounds, I will sell it for six thousand pounds. This is how money comes!"

"How much did you pay for it?" the man asked.

Amin answered, "I bought it for . . ." He was about to say, "two thousand pounds." But the ring gave him such a prick, that for a time he thought it was a snake or a scorpion. He gave such a cry that the man jumped back. Then Amin remembered the ring. "One hundred pounds is the price. Therefore you will pay me three hundred pounds."

Yet each day after that Amin told himself, "If I had just disobeyed the ring, I would have had six thousand pounds more for that piece of cloth. This is a cursed luck."

Late one afternoon, as he was swimming in the Nile, he said to himself, "If I, now, cry that I am about to be drowned, my friends will rush to come and help me and save me from drowning. When they are near, and about to save me, I will go under the water, as if I have sunk forever, swim toward the bank, and then come to the surface and laugh at them. This will be a funny trick and a joke to make us laugh for a long time to come."

When he was about to cry out, Amin thought that a crocodile had caught his left hand, because the prick of the ring was so severe and hard to endure. He knew that he had planned to lie, to cause others trouble. So he did not do what he had intended to do.

Time went on and Amin was known to be as good as his father. Some people said that he was even better than his father.

The devil, whose name in Arabic is Shaytan, was not pleased at all. He had a meeting with all his sons and helpers and discussed the matter with them. All of them came to the conclusion that wine and money would turn Amin's morals upside down.

Wine is prohibited in Islam. It is often called the mother of the worst evil. One is not allowed to drink even a little bit of anything that, if consumed in large quantities, will make one drunk.

Shaytan, in the form of a rich man, came into Amin's shop. He chose a piece of cloth, and told Amin that he would pay six times the price Amin had paid for it.

Amin had bought it for fifty pounds, but said that he had paid a thousand pounds for it. The ring gave him such a prick that Amin gave a cry that made his customer step back, thinking that the merchant was going to die of pain from a snake bite.

But Amin took six thousand pounds and a ring bite for that piece of cloth, instead of the three hundred pounds he was supposed to receive.

The next day Shaytan appeared in the same shape as the previous day. He said that his wife had liked that piece of cloth and thought the price to be very low. He also insisted that the good trader should come for supper that evening. Shaytan chose a piece of cloth worth only twenty pounds, and promised to give Amin ten times its price. Amin said that he had bought it for a thousand pounds. Here the ring gave Amin a sharp sting, but not as severe as the last one. Shaytan told Amin that his prices were very low. He paid ten thousand pounds and told Amin that he would come and take him to supper in the evening. Amin promised to come another evening, but not that one.

Every day Shaytan came and bought a new piece of cloth for a very high price, and every day he told Amin that his prices were very low. The pricks of the ring grew less and less severe each time.

Amin and Shaytan became friends and began to go out together to different places. In most of those places there was gambling, bad women, and wine. In the course of time Amin learned every bad thing. He became a drunkard and a gambler and went from the arms of one woman to another.

Amin began to hate poor people and good men. He also noticed that the pricks of the ring became milder and milder, until he felt them no more. In the end, Amin did every bad thing without feeling a prick at all.

He was now an addict, a miser, and a liar. His work deteriorated. Nobody came to buy from him or sell to him. His closest friend, Shaytan, disappeared. He was nowhere to be found. Even the houses that he used to take Amin to disappeared, as if they were swallowed and went underground. Time went on and Amin went from bad to worse.

One day Amin visited his father and told him everything. The father was both sorry and sad for his only son. Together they worked hard; they prayed, they tried to be always with Allah as He was always with them.

Amin, step by step, slowly stopped gambling, drinking, and going with many women, and instead used his mind for prayer. His conscience returned to him. He became a good man again, thanks to his father and the lessons he had learned from the bite of the ring.

THE NABAGA OF LIFE

In centuries past, hundreds of years ago, when the world was full of Rhooles and evil spirits, and when all things—trees, birds, Rhooles, and people—used to speak the same language, there lived Fatma the Beautiful and her three brave brothers.

Their father and mother had died a long time ago. They lived in the town of the sultan. (Really there is no Sultan except the creator of the universe.) The sultan was very cruel, unjust, and miserly.

Fatma the Beautiful had three things. First, when she laughed, jewels, pearls, and gold came out of her mouth. Second, when she walked, the moment she took her foot off the ground fragrant flowers and beautiful roses appeared where her foot had been. Every step brought sweet-smelling flowers in beautiful colors. Third, if ever she wept, the rains came.

Her house was at the end of the town of the sultan. As she was the most beautiful among all the girls, the sultan (and there is no Sultan except the creator of the universe) asked her brothers to allow him to marry their sister, Fatma the Beautiful. But, because he was cruel, and because they were really not afraid of anyone, they refused. He tried by all means to marry that beautiful girl, but he could not.

There was a witch near his palace. He called her and said, "O witch! If you make me marry Fatma the Beautiful, I will give you anything you want." She said to him, "Build me a small house near her house." So a house was built and the old witch lived in that house.

She began to visit Fatma the Beautiful from time to time, and she helped Fatma in every way. She was very kind to Fatma, and Fatma and her brothers loved that witch very much, not knowing that she was a wicked witch sent by the sultan.

When they were acquainted with each other and had become very friendly, the witch asked Fatma, "Do your brothers love you very much?"

Fatma said, "Of course they do. They love me dearly. You see how they always go into the forest, hunt animals for me, and bring me anything I like."

The witch said to her, "Did they bring you the nabaga of life?" (The nabaga is a small, very sweet, Sudanese fruit from the sidir tree.)

Fatma asked, "The nabaga of life? I have never heard of that before."

The witch said to her, "O! It is a special nabaga. Anyone who eats it lives forever." Then the witch went home.

Fatma was astonished that her brothers had not brought her that nabaga. So she began to weep. Her weeping brought the rain, and her brothers, in the forest, were afraid that something bad had happened to their sister. So they rode their horses and came to her. They found her weeping.

"What is the matter?" they asked.

Fatma said, "I thought that you loved me very much."

"But we do," they said.

"Why, then, did you not bring me the nabaga of life?" she asked.

"What! The nabaga of life? We never heard of it," they replied.

She said, "It is a nabaga which, when eaten by anyone, gives eternal life."

The brothers immediately promised to go and bring her that nabaga.

But the eldest brother, Basheer, said, "I am the eldest and I must go. I will come back soon." He mounted his horse and rode away.

On his way, Basheer met an old woman. She was terribly thirsty and hungry. He had enough food and water. She begged him for some. He gave her food and water. Then she asked where he was going, and he told her. She told him he was going to a dangerous place, where the most unlikely things would talk to him. He must not reply to them. Basheer thanked her and traveled on.

His brothers and sister waited, day after day, week after week, month after month, until they had waited a complete year. Basheer did not come back. So the middle brother, Hamza, traveled.

Hamza met the same old woman. She gave him the same warning. He too disappeared. Days passed, weeks passed, months passed, a year passed, but he did not come back.

Finally the youngest brother, Awad, said to his sister, "Well, Fatma the Beautiful, I am going to bring you the nabaga and find my brothers." She begged him not to go, but he insisted.

Awad had very little food and water. He became thirsty and hungry. Then he saw something lying in the desert, on the horizon, where the sky seemed to meet the earth.

He went to the thing and saw that it was a very old woman dying of hunger and thirst. She begged him for water. He was thirsty and hungry, but the woman was about to die. Awad gave her all the food and water he had and she blessed him. He traveled on.

Then he met another woman. This woman was healthy. She asked him where he was going. He said to her, "I am going to find my two brothers and to bring the nabaga of life to my sister."

The woman said to him, "Because you are a generous man, and you have given me your last drop of water and last bit of food, I will help you."

He said to her, "But I have not met you before." She told him that she was the old woman he had met earlier, to whom he had given his last food and water.

She said to him, "When you go, you will come to a giant. Each of his legs will be on a mountain. A river runs under him, between his legs. He has a huge sword, great and tall as the minaret of a mosque. He will ask you things and you must answer him this way." Then she told him what to tell the giant.

"When you go further, you will find robbers," she continued. "Scatter this money on the ground in front of them. They will try to collect the money and you can avoid them and go on. You will come to a huge army of dangerous ants: scatter this sugar in front of them and then you can pass. Then you will come across a fierce lion: drop this sheep and pass on your way avoiding the lion, which will be eating the sheep. After that you will arrive at a huge door. Knock on it three times only! The door will open. Go through it and you will find beautiful flowers. They will greet you, but you must not answer them! When you enter you will find many statues of stone and marble, all of human beings and beautifully built. Then you will come to an island encircled by deep water. On the island is a beautiful, huge green sidir tree with only one nabaga, the nabaga of life. This fruit appears only once a year. Five large, fierce birds with sharp teeth are waiting on the tree for the nabaga to ripen and turn red. They will fight for the nabaga, and only one will survive the fight. The other four will die in the battle.

"Take these seven seeds with you. When you arrive at the water you will find a swan as big as a camel, swimming in the water. Ask her to take you across to the island. She will refuse. Show her one of the seven seeds, and tell her if she takes you to the island you will give it to her.

"Take this pair of flying shoes, that will carry you in the air in time of need. And take this sword—it has heavenly blades that can kill any opponent."

He thanked her and took a boat on the river. He saw the giant, whose head reached the clouds, carrying the sword the old woman had warned him about. Each of the giant's legs rested on one of the mountains, with the river running between them. His sword was as large as the minaret of a mosque, and he swung it right and left, up and down.

In a loud, fearful voice, the giant asked Awad where he was going. Awad replied that he was going to bring the nabaga of life to his sister and to try to find his two brothers. The giant told him that he couldn't pass unless he answered a question. "What is it?" asked Awad.

"There is a thing that walks on four legs in the morning, on two at noon, and on three in the evening. What is it?"

Awad thought and thought. "O, I know, it is a human being. As a baby, he crawls on his hands and knees. Then he learns to walk on his two legs alone. But when he is very old he helps his two legs with a stick and walks on three." The giant was pleased and let the young man pass.

After that Awad left the boat and rode his horse, carrying the things that were given to him by the old woman. On his horse, he crossed mountains, forests, deserts, and rivers.

Suddenly he saw robbers who came dashing at him with their swords, trying to kill him. He took out the sack full of money and scattered the money in all directions as far as he could. The robbers all ran after the money, and he passed them in peace.

He did not go far before he found an army of ants that stretched for miles in every direction. They made fearful noises. He poured the sugar and the ants busied themselves eating and collecting the sugar. So he passed them, too.

Suddenly his horse stopped. The fiercest lion Awad had ever seen was coming toward him. Its claws were like swords and its teeth like knives. Awad put the sheep in the lion's path. The lion didn't hesitate. Finding a sheep in front of him, he attacked it and began to eat it, allowing the young man to pass.

Then he saw a wall with a huge wooden door. He reached for it and knocked exactly three times, as the old woman had told him to do. The door opened.

Oh, what a beautiful place! Lofty fruit trees, beautiful flowers, and roses that filled the air with the sweetest scent. He forgot all his hunger, thirst, and fatigue. He was full of new life and hope. Entering that paradise, he heard every bit of everything greeting him. He was so happy that, for a moment, he was about to reply their greetings, but fortunately he remembered the old woman's warning: "Don't answer them!" So he went on without replying to their greetings.

He arrived at the bank of the river and saw an island there with one green tree in the middle of it. In the top branches he could see very strong birds. He had never seen their kind before. A big swan came swimming quickly towards him, as if it was going to swallow him. Awad stepped back. The swan stopped at the bank. He asked her to carry him to the island across the river, but she refused. He showed her one of the seeds and told her, if she took him to the island, he would give her the seed. No sooner had he told her than she agreed to carry him.

He rode on her back to the island. He gave her the seed, went to the sidir tree, and sat in the shade. He was very, very tired. He looked up at the five birds. They were gigantic, fearful, and strong, with sharp teeth in their beaks.

The ripening nabaga slowly changed from green to yellow. The birds were ready to fight. They made loud noises. They used their wings to hit each other, opening their fearful, wide mouths, and showing their sharp teeth.

The nabaga was on the lowest branch. Awad watched as it changed colors. The quarrel between the birds became fiercer. The nabaga became bright yellow. Then it turned red. All the birds flew toward it. Awad took the five seeds, which were redder than the nabaga, and threw them far away. The birds changed direction to fly after the seeds. They left the nabaga.

Awad quickly picked the nabaga, ran to the swan, and showed her the remaining seventh seed. She agreed to take him across to the other bank.

Reaching there, he didn't forget to take a good quantity of water. He had been told by the woman to take water from the river, dip his finger in it, and put his finger on each of the statues he found there. So he did that. Every time he dipped his finger in the water and put it on a statue, the statue changed into a man or a woman.

They had all been changed into statues the moment they replied to the greetings of the trees, flowers, roses, and grass. He changed them back into people. In the middle, there were two statues near each other. They were his two brothers, Basheer and Hamza. You can't imagine their pleasure.

Among the changed statues there was a beautiful princess and a brave smart prince. They were brother and sister. There were also two exceptionally beautiful sisters.

Awad asked the princess to marry him and she agreed. Her brother agreed to marry Fatma the Beautiful. His two brothers and the two beautiful sisters agreed to marry each other.

They all started for home, beginning their backward journey.

When they were near their town, heavy rains came. This was because their sister was weeping. Awad put on his winged flying shoes, took his sword, and flew to their house. Entering the house, he did not find Fatma, but instead found the witch in an ugly state. Her hair stood on end, her teeth were like spears, her eyes were red and as big as cups, and her nose was like a water jug. Her nails were as long as knives and, moreover, she had a tail.

He asked where his sister was. The witch said she wouldn't tell him. With one strike of his sword her head came down. But another head grew in its place, and the head that was cut said to him, "Do you think I am the only head?"

The young man said, "Do you think my blade is one?" He delivered another blow. The second head ran around on the ground crying, "Do you think we are only two heads?" A third head came out in place of the previous one. Again Awad said that the blades of his sword were not two. He cut off the third head. A fourth head came out. Every time he cut off a head, another grew in its place. He cut off six heads.

The seventh head appeared and said that she would tell him the location of his sister if he would promise not to cut the last head. He promised. The witch told him that his sister was taken by the sultan, who was trying to marry her. They were at a feast attended by many kings and princes, queens and princesses. Awad flew to the sultan's palace and found it full of life. People were singing and dancing. Kings, queens, princes, princesses, and great men of different kingdoms were attending the feast and marriage.

He went to the sultan and demanded that his sister be set free. The sultan refused. Each took out his sword and a fight began. After a short battle, the sultan was killed. All the people rejoiced, because the sultan was very cruel, miserly, and unjust. Awad was appointed the new sultan.

His brothers, the princess, the prince, and the two beautiful girls arrived. The prince and princess found their father. The two girls were princesses, too, and they found their father there.

Each of the boys married a princess. The prince married Fatma the Beautiful. Awad married the princess and the feast continued for fifteen days.

All were happy. They had many sons and daughters. They lived a long, happy life until death came upon them.

THE FATAL
BEAUTY OF TAJOUJ

The Humran tribe has long lived on the border of eastern Sudan. The girls of the Humran tribe are known all over the Sudan to have the most beautiful bodies. Their faces are like the moon; their eyes are black and wide as cups; their necks are delicate, like the bottles that are made in Istanbul. They are the most beautiful girls.

Among the Humran girls was Tajouj. She was the most beautiful girl ever known. She was taller than all the girls of the Humran tribe. Her hair was very black and long, her body was like the color of wheat. Her teeth were as white as milk.

Al Mahalag was her neighbor. He was the best of all the men of the tribe. He was strong, brave, generous, smart, and from one of the richest families.

When they grew to adulthood, Al Mahalag and Tajouj were married to each other. Al Mahalag was the happiest man in his tribe, which was the happiest among all the neighboring tribes.

Al Mahalag had a friend named Ahmed. Ahmed was also a smart, brave, generous man, and his family was as great as those of Al Mahalag and Tajouj. He had a very beautiful wife called Asia. Asia was not equal to Tajouj in beauty, although she was more beautiful than all the rest of the girls of the Humran tribe. Still Ahmed was sad, because he had heard that Tajouj was more beautiful than Asia, his wife. He was sad that he had not married Tajouj.

Ahmed envied Al Mahalag. He envied him for all his talents, his family, his riches, his generosity, his bravery, and, above all, for his wife Tajouj, the most beautiful of all the girls. He envied everything Al Mahalag had.

One day Ahmed visited Al Mahalag in his house and spoke to him. "My dear friend, we have been friends a long time, and our custom in the village, among the tribe, is that when a girl is married, she dances naked, as naked as the day her mother gave birth to her. When I married, you saw my wife dance naked, but I didn't see your wife. People say that Tajouj is the most beautiful girl, while I think that my wife, Asia, is more beautiful than your wife."

Each said that his wife was more beautiful than the other's wife.

Al Mahalag then called for Tajouj to come. When she entered the room, he introduced her to his friend. "Tajouj! Meet my friend, Ahmed."

Tajouj greeted Ahmed in a hurried way and ran out of the room very shyly. Girls of the tribe are very shy when meeting men who are not close relatives.

Ahmed saw a beautiful face; he had never dreamed that there was such beauty in this life. He saw the face, but he didn't see the rest of the body, because she was wearing her garment and the Sudanese *toab*, her sari.

Ahmed asked to see Tajouj naked as Al Mahalag had seen Asia naked in her marriage dance. In some tribal places people, on the marriage night, climb trees or walls and look at the bride, through the window, dancing to the bridegroom and her bridesmaids, wearing nothing but a small *rahat* (a fringed leather belt) around her waist. This happens before the entry night.

The entry night is the night when the wife is brought to her husband's room, where they sleep together for the first time. That is the first time they find themselves alone in their private room, where they begin their family life.

Although this was not Al Mahalag's first night living with his wife, he asked Ahmed to come at night and watch Tajouj dancing or walking naked so that he would be sure that there was nobody alive as beautiful as Tajouj. Ahmed would climb a tree just outside and look through the window of their room.

That night when Tajouj came to the room to sleep, Al Mahalag

72

said to her, "Tajouj, I want you to walk naked from the door to the window."

She got very angry and said to him, "You know this is forbidden by religion and by human law." He answered that it was a known custom among the tribe and every woman did it, when asked by her man.

She was both sad and angry. She said to him, "I'll do it under one condition: that you grant me a wish." He said that he would grant her anything she wished, even if that wish was his life. Tajouj insisted that both his and her parents must attend to the agreement between them.

The parents came and were told about the agreement. They agreed to it and then went out.

Tajouj obeyed. She took off her clothes, piece by piece, until she was as naked as when she was born.

Weeping tears as great as rain, she walked from the door to the window. Very quickly she put on her clothes again.

Ahmed, who was on a very high branch of a tree just outside the window, saw beauty that he had never dreamed existed in this life. He fell down from that height, broke his neck, and died instantly.

Tajouj, after putting on her clothes, sent for the parents to come. She said, "I did what he demanded. Now ask him about that, isn't it true?"

He answered in the affirmative, and said, "What is your wish? If you want my soul it is yours."

She answered, "I don't want your soul. I want you to divorce me, and now."

Al Mahalag and the parents were astonished to hear that. Everyone knew that the love between those two was unlike any before it. He didn't want to divorce her. The ground began to move from under his legs. He was about to faint. He wanted to refuse, but a promise is a promise.

A man must keep his promise, especially among the Humran tribe. He divorced her.

He became a miserably unhappy man. His mind was always full of Tajouj, the love between them, and how that happiness ended. He began to wander from street to street and then out of the village from valley to valley and from one hill to another. He sat under the trees and talked to them of his lost paradise. He made up songs about Tajouj. Very sad songs they were. He was comparing his past life and all its happiness with how he now lived.

The wise old people of the village were not at all happy about what had happened. They chose a man from among them and asked him to try to remedy the situation. He went to both parents and asked that Tajouj be remarried to Al Mahalag.

Now, when someone is in love with a girl, and wants to marry her, one must never make up songs about her, describing her beauty or telling how deeply he loves her. If this happens they will never be married to each other. The moment one makes up a single verse, the girl's family will not allow any marriage between the two, because making up songs about a special girl is considered immoral.

The parents didn't allow the remarriage to take place, because they had heard the songs Al Mahalag sang about Tajouj. The wise man told the parents that since the couple was married to each other before, Al Mahalag was singing the songs about his ex-wife. The law did not apply.

If Tajouj was not shy, and if it had been the custom for girls of her tribe to speak frankly, she would have said that she wanted to remarry her ex-husband.

At last the parents accepted the remarriage, on condition that not a single song be sung by Al Mahalag.

That old wise man rode on his camel and went looking for Al Mahalag. At last, after many days and nights, he found him, ragged, thirsty, hungry, and very thin. He told him what the parents' conditions were for his remarriage: he must not sing any song about Tajouj until they were remarried. This was very important; if he failed to abide by it, they could not remarry.

All the universe could not carry him, because of his happiness. They mounted their camels and began their return journey.

The man was very busy talking to Al Mahalag, trying his best to keep Al Mahalag from thinking about Tajouj. The man asked Al Mahalag all sorts of questions about the places they came through: villages, mountains, forests, and valleys. At night he asked him about all the stars they saw: their names, when they came out, when they disappeared.

He asked about the history of the tribe and the most important incidents that had happened. He also engaged himself in telling Al Mahalag many, many other things.

He did not give him any time to think of Tajouj. He tried his best not to give him a single moment to sing one single verse about Tajouj. They rode on and on. The first night passed, and the man was pleased that nothing happened.

The second night passed peacefully; not a word was said about Tajouj.

On the third day the man was trying hard to divert Al Mahalag's attention away from the village, his parents, all the people of the village, and, above all, from his memories of Tajouj.

Still they rode on. The man drove the camels as hard as he could. It was now dawn and at sunset they would arrive at their destination.

From a far away village, at that silent hour of dawn, Al Mahalag heard a cock crying for the prayer of dawn. The cock was crowing to awaken people for their prayers.

Cocks and hens sometimes sleep on ropes stretched from wall to wall or from tree to tree to hang the wash. The poor animals must constantly shift and move about to keep their balance, and they do not get much rest. That is why people who are having difficulties say that they are sleeping like a cock on a rope.

Hearing the cocks, Al Mahalag remembered his condition without Tajouj and how unhappy he was. He sang a song in which he said that a cock sleeping comfortably on the rope with the hens is happier than he himself without Tajouj.

"Oh! Why did you say that?" said Al Mahalag's companion. "My agreement with the elders and with your parents is of no use. This is the end. You ought not to have sung this song about Tajouj."

Now Al Mahalag knew that all his dreams about remarrying Tajouj were of no use after what he had done. That was the end. He took a deep breath, fell from the camel, and died.

Tajouj was waiting for him, because she loved him dearly. But they brought her his dead body instead.

Time passed, months followed months and another tribe made war on the Humran tribe and defeated it. Tajouj was taken captive by that tribe. Her beauty was the cause of many catastrophes. Every man of that tribe wanted to marry her. Fights broke out between men of the same tribe. Many killings took place. Every man who advanced to marry her was killed by another one.

An old man saw that Tajouj caused many deaths and that there was no end to the deaths. Tajouj would ruin the tribe by her beauty. He decided to get rid of her.

One day at dusk the man took his bow and only one arrow, hid under a bush near Tajouj's tent, and called her. She came out to see who was calling her. The man took a sure aim at her breast and sent the arrow through the air. It struck Tajouj in the heart. She fell dead.

WHAT BRAVERY IS

In a small town that grew up on the bank of the river called the White Nile lived Musa, who was known for his generosity. He had a very large *khalwa*, a room for the social life of the people of the village or town. All the people of the village brought their meals to the *khalwa* and ate collectively. The rich and the poor did that, especially when they had a guest or guests who were on their way to other places. Everybody brought what he could afford. Travelers all over the Sudan came to these *khalwas* to stay and rest for a day or two before resuming their journeys. The villagers hosted them as long as they stayed. Some *khalwas* were always filled with guests. Because of this, all the villagers or townspeople brought all their meals to the *khalwas*, and served as hosts for the guests.

Sometimes a rich, generous man or a religious man hosted all the guests alone. The people of the village could come, eat with the guests, enjoy their meals, and enjoy the company of the guests.

Musa was rich, generous, and a man of religion. That was why his *khalwa* was the destination of every guest who came in that direction.

People were always talking about Musa, his good behavior and his love of guests. He, every now and then, told his sons, friends, and followers that whenever he spent a single cent on a guest, Allah gave him much more in return than he had spent. He said to them, "The trade that brings the best profit is what one spends on one's guests. It profits one now and in the hereafter. Whenever one can spend money

77

on the poor or on one's guests, one will find that multiplied, but one must do it privately, only to please Allah."

People always talked about the pleasure Musa found in spending money on those in need. They told that he shivered, shook, and trembled when he was helping people. Those were the signs of deep generosity and bravery.

His fame traveled all over the country. Everybody heard of him and wished to be like him. People in the east, west, north, south, and center spoke of no one as they spoke of Musa. They had nothing to talk about that could equal Musa's generosity.

Many women all around the White Nile region called their newborn sons Musa, in hope that they would grow up to be like him.

Now, at that same time, it happened that there lived a very brave strong man in the northern region of the country. His village lay on the bank of the great River Nile. His name was Salih.

Salih rode his horse from village to village. Whenever he found a man or woman who was treated unjustly, he did all that he could to bring justice.

Sometimes miserly rulers enlarged their lands by annexing lands owned by the poor or weak, or those lacking strength or vigor. Those poor people always went to Salih for help. Salih would be sure to see that their lands were returned to them.

Many times he was even compelled to use his sword, to make sure that justice was done. One day a man told him that he was attacked by robbers on his way to another town to sell his goods. There were about fifteen robbers that attacked traders on the highway, and all the caravans suffered these attacks. The merchant's goods had been carried on twenty camels. Salih, on the back of his camel, began to trace the tracks of the robbers in the desert.

Salih found the hiding place of the robbers after a wearying trip that took him many days and nights. They were in the middle of the desert in a small village surrounded by many mountains. He asked them to give him the stolen goods of the merchant. They refused. Salih got out his sword and a fight was about to begin, when one of the thieves recognized him. He said to his men, "Look here, men.

This man is Salih. If he defeats us, then we are dead men. But if we could kill him, and this I don't think will happen, then we will bury bravery forever. I think we had better give him what he wants."

He was given all the goods. Then he said to them, "Your leader is wise. He knows when to act peacefully. I tell you that I can defeat you if your number is multiplied by three. But this is not the important thing. The important thing is that you take from people the things they tired themselves to collect. Don't you feel ashamed when you do such an evil thing? Why don't you begin a new honest life, instead of living away from other people and just appearing at night like bats to cause trouble and death to good people?" It is said that all those thieves then became good citizens.

People said that Salih could defeat a whole army. His fame traveled from place to place, all across the country. Everyone who needed help, and could get in touch with him, was helped.

Like Musa on the White Nile, his name was given by every mother to her baby son. The name Salih was found in many places at that time. Every woman hoped that her child would be like Salih.

Each man's fame reached the other. Musa wanted very much to befriend Salih. Salih, too, wanted to know Musa. Each one of them was eager to see the other.

Years passed. Musa began a northward journey to meet Salih. At the same time, Salih began a long journey southward to see Musa. Each one was hoping to develop a friendship with the other.

Musa always hoped to be as brave as he was generous. Salih also wanted to be as generous as he was brave. Each one of them wanted to have these two virtues and the commendable qualities that accompany them. Bravery and generosity were valued by both men. They wanted very much to befriend one another and learn from one another. That was why each of them began his hard journey to the other. Journeys were very difficult at that time, and the shortest journey might take days, if not weeks. The journey which each of the two men began would take more than two months.

After some weeks of travel, each of the travelers thought of resting for a few days at the first possible opportunity. Salih found a forest. He entered the forest to take his rest under the lofty, thick trees.

Under a big thick tree, with long branches that stretched for several yards in all directions, he found a man. That man was Musa. Neither knew the other. They greeted one another very warmly. It was a custom at that time that no one should ask a stranger a direct question about his name, or from where he had come. In the course of time and during conversations between people, those things would become known. If, after three days, those things were not known, then questions would be accepted and answered.

When lunch time came, Musa said to Salih, "I will divorce my wife if we ever take a grain of your food. I will divorce my wife unless you will be my guest as long as we stay together."

Some people used to say, "I will divorce my wife," instead of "I swear." These were the strongest possible words, ones that must be obeyed, otherwise it would be necessary to divorce one's wife. One was always obeyed when one said, "I will divorce my wife." So they ate from Musa's food all the time. It was healthy and rich food. Musa served the meals as well. Salih was pleased by the food as well as Musa's generosity and his readiness to help and serve his guest.

Some robbers heard that Musa was carrying a great amount of money with him and that he was traveling alone. They decided to attack him and steal the money.

The next day, just before sunset, the two men were attacked by robbers. Before the fight took place Salih said to Musa, "I will divorce my wife if you take up your sword against these nasty rats. You just rest and watch." Taking his weapon, riding his horse and attacking the thieves, Salih wounded many of the robbers in a short time. Then the others took their wounded and ran.

Musa was pleased. He admired his friend's bravery and strength. But he did not know who his friend was. On the third day each began to ask about the other's destination, their places, and their names. When Musa asked Salih where he was going, Salih said to him, "I have heard of Musa, the generous man of the White Nile. I want to visit him, find the truth of what people say about him, and learn how to be as generous a man as he is."

Musa asked, "Don't you know him? Haven't you ever seen him?" Salih answered in the negative. Then Musa told his friend that he was Musa. Salih cried out, "I have seen your generosity in not allowing me to give you any of my food, in providing all the food for both of us. But tell me, how did you become that generous? What is the cause of your fame? Tell me how to become generous myself, because, if there is only one thing I desire, it is to be as generous as you are."

Musa answered, "Whenever a guest comes to me, I put myself in his place and imagine what I would like the host to do for me. Everything that I imagine, I do for the guest. In this way I have become known for my generosity."

Then Salih asked Musa where he was going. Musa answered, "You heard of my generosity and took all the difficulties of trying to reach me at my home to learn how to be generous. You are a good man and I am sure that your relation with Allah is sincere. That is why he brought me here to you, before you had to endure the difficulties of traveling to my far village. But I still have a very long way to go. I have heard, as has everyone in the country, of the bravery of Salih. I am going to Salih to learn how to be brave. And if I become both brave and generous, then I won't want anything else in this world. I am going to see Salih."

Salih answered, "Now look here, Musa! Poverty is the worst enemy a man can face. Everybody is afraid of poverty, even Salih, whom you are going to see. The man who gives all his money to the needy, he who gives food to everyone without being afraid of being poor, he who does all these things is the bravest man. You don't need to go to Salih."

Musa answered, "I will divorce my wife if I don't see him. I shall never go back home, even if I die on the road."

Finding that Musa was determined and resolute to see Salih, Salih said to him, "I am Salih." They greeted each other warmly and saluted one another. Each was very pleased. Salih said to Musa, "Allah loves you. That is why he brought me to you in the middle of the road, instead of making you go all the distance to my village on the other side of the wide River Nile in the far north. What do you ask."

Musa answered, "I want to know how you became so brave."

Salih said to Musa, "I want you to put your finger in my mouth, between my teeth, and I will put my finger between your teeth. You begin to bite me and I will begin to bite you." Each put his finger between the teeth of the other and each began to bite. Time passed. Each continued biting the other. After some time, Musa cried out in pain. Each let go of the other's finger.

Salih said to his friend, "I was suffering the same pain. It ached me as it did you. If you hadn't cried I would have cried myself. You just cried before I did. I was only more patient than you. Bravery is only patience."

THE WICKED BROTHER

Once in past days, a long time ago, a man lived with his beautiful wife, his son, and his daughter.

The man was very rich. He was a merchant, who traveled in a caravan and moved from town to town, from country to country, selling his goods and buying new goods, making a good profit. After a long journey, he would come home with his earnings. He had a wicked, miserly, and brutal brother, with whom he shared all his profits, even though his brother didn't deserve it.

Every year the man went on his long journey, until one year his wife died. Then he didn't travel for a time, trying to look after his son and his daughter, and bring them up wisely.

When he was ready to journey again, he took his son and daughter to his brother, their uncle, and said to him, "Oh, brother, I'm going on my journey and the boy and the girl don't have anyone to look after them. I want you to look after them until I come back." The uncle agreed, and the father went off in a caravan.

When the rainy season came, the uncle opened the store of his absent brother, the merchant, and took sacks of corn to plant on his plantation.

He made his brother's son and daughter work for him. They planted all his land with corn. They looked after it. He gave them no food. He clothed them no more.

They were very unhappy. But they had a cow. Whenever their uncle was not there, they went to the cow and said to her, "Oh cow of

our mother and our father, give us milk." The cow would give them milk, because she looked upon them as if they were her own calves.

The two children spent a great part of every night weeping and remembering their dead mother and their absent father.

The corn grew tall, bearing very large ears. The merchant's brother was very miserly and very wicked. He would count all the ears of corn every day. And he always said to the children, "If one of you takes any corn, I will kill you both."

The boy was very hungry and his sister was very hungry; they were about to die. Their uncle would not give them any food. He would not allow them to take any corn. Day after day they felt hungry, and hungry, and hungry.

Finally they were too hungry to think about what their uncle would do to them if they ate an ear of corn. So the boy chose a very big ear of corn, cooked it, and ate it with his sister. Being afraid of their uncle, they dug a deep hole in the ground, buried the remainder of their meal of corn, and filled the hole with dirt.

A short time later their uncle arrived. He was astonished to see that they were lively. He began to count the ears of corn one by one. At last he came to the plant where one of the ears was missing!

When he asked them about it, they answered that a sparrow had eaten it, flown away, and crossed the seven seas. The uncle was very angry, because he was very miserly and did not want to lose even one kernel of corn. He took his knife, caught the boy, Mohammed, and killed him.

Batoul, Mohammed's sister, began to run, after seeing her brother get killed. Her uncle ran after her. She entered the forest where all the wild beasts lived.

The uncle was afraid of the wild beasts, so he went back, sure that Batoul would be eaten by the beasts. But Batoul went on, running and running and running. The thorns tore her clothes and cut into her skin, but still she ran on until she came to a road on the other side of the forest. She came out of the forest. Far away she saw dust. She waited.

A caravan of merchants came. She asked about her father in a song.

O caravan, isn't my father with you?
He is green and tall. (A green man means a brown man in Sudanese speech.)
His garment is made of silk.
His camel is always crying, because of his strength.
His whip makes a sound in the air.
My uncle, the brother of my father, killed my brother, Mohammed,
Because of an ear of corn that was eaten by a sparrow that crossed the seven seas.

The song runs like this in Arabic:

Ya jallaba ma fiecum abuy,
Akhader utaweel,
Tobu tobe hareer,
Jamalul hiddeer,
Sotul wirweer,
Ammi khay abouy,
Gatal Mohammed akhouy,
Ashan gandoul
Wal gandoul,
Nagadu zarzour,
Utar beh fi saba'a bhur.

The leader of the caravan said to her, "Your father is in the next caravan." She waited.

Another caravan came and again she asked about her father, singing the same song.

Again the leader of the caravan answered that her father was with the next caravan. A third caravan came, and the same thing happened, then a fourth, a fifth, and a sixth without any result.

Then she saw her uncle running toward her with his knife in his hand. The next caravan was far away on the horizon, where the sky seemed to touch the earth.

Her uncle came running toward her. She ran for her life.

He was gaining. When he was about to catch her, she cried to the ground under her feet, "Oh earth, hide me from my uncle, please!"

The ground opened and the girl went into it and the ground closed again.

The uncle waited and waited and waited.

When Batoul was sure that the caravan had come, she asked the earth to open. The earth opened and she stood just in front of the leader of the caravan.

She sang again.

> O caravan isn't my father with you?
> He is green and tall,
> His garment is made of silk,
> His camel is always crying, because of his strength,
> His whip makes a sound in the air,
> My uncle, the brother of my father, killed my brother,
> Mohammed,
> Because of an ear of corn that was eaten by a sparrow that
> crossed the seven seas.

Her father was among the people in that caravan. He heard her voice, and said, "Again girl! Sing that again."

Batoul sang the verses again and her father appeared.

When the uncle saw his brother, the father of Mohammed and Batoul, he ran for his life. His brother ran after him.

When he was sure that his brother was close enough to catch him, being very afraid of death the uncle cried to the ground, "Oh ground, open and hide me from my brother, who wants to kill me." He did not even say, "PLEASE." The earth did not open. It refused. He was a bad man. He ought to be killed. The ground refused to open, because it did not want to save a cruel criminal.

He went on running and running. But his brother at last caught him. The father of Mohammed and Batoul killed his brother and burned his body. The ashes were carried away by the wind, because the earth refused to keep even his ashes.

IN UNITY
THERE IS STRENGTH

T he Butana is a large area that lies to the east of the river known as the Blue Nile and extends to the boundaries of Ethiopia, Eritrea, and the Atbara River to the River Nile near the city of Shendi. This land is inhabited by many tribes under the rule of the Shukria tribe.

At one time the senior ruler was Sheikh Abu Ali (whose name means "the father of Ali"), who was a wise and just leader. He was generous, brave, and always looked kindly upon the poor and tried to help and serve them. He was loved by all the people of the Butana. He had ten sons, whom he brought up and educated in the Qur'an school of the village. He asked the best *Faqih* (the name given to a teacher of the Qur'an) to stay in the village and teach the boys.

All the village boys went to the Qur'an school. They learned the Qur'an and the proper life of the good Muslim. The sons of the Sheikh grew up to be wise, clever, brave, and generous.

The Sheikh grew older and older. One day he became ill. *Baseers* (healers) came from the big city and returned there. Many medicines were given to him. Every *baseer* tried his best to cure the Sheikh, but all were unsuccessful.

The eldest son, Ali, went to Khartoum, the capital, to bring the best *baseer* available. The *baseer* went to Sheikh Abu Ali. He saw to it that the Sheikh had good medicines and a good diet. The Sheikh took all the medicines and followed the diet carefully. He began to feel better.

Every day he improved. The people were happy, for he began to recover. Then one day, suddenly, his health failed. He was in pain all over his body. He was sure that his end was near.

He called his sons to a meeting. He asked each to bring his camel-driving stick with him and to bring a second stick as well. They brought their sticks and stood in front of their dying father, waiting for his orders. He asked each of them to break his stick. They did so easily. Then he asked the youngest son to collect the ten unbroken sticks and tie them with a rope. The boy obeyed.

Now the Sheikh asked this son to break the tied bundle of sticks. The boy tried to break them, but he could not. He tried harder, but it was impossible.

The Sheikh asked his youngest son to give the sticks to his elder brother. When given the sticks, he was asked by his father to break them. The elder son tried even harder, but it was useless.

The second son was asked to give the bundle of sticks to his elder, third brother, who also failed to break them, no matter how hard he tried.

The bundle of sticks moved from brother to brother. Each one used his utmost strength trying to break the sticks, but it could not be done. No one could break the tied sticks.

The eldest son, number ten, Ali, who was known for his great strength, also tried, but failed. He couldn't break them.

At last the Sheikh, with labored breathing, asked Ali to put the bundle of sticks on the other bed. The young man did so. With weary eyes and tired tongue the Sheikh said to them, "My sons, I am passing away. I am dying. I think I have brought you up well. I have given you an education and taught you how to live honorable lives. Your eldest brother, Ali, will now carry on my duties toward the people. He will serve them, I hope better than I have done. Obey him! Look upon him as your new father! Be good to him! Serve him and help him to serve our people! And you, Ali, look upon your brothers as I looked upon you! Be a father to them. My sons, you must all serve the people of the Butana. Be their servants and don't be their masters! If you promise me that, I will pass away happy and with a light heart."

The sons all promised their father everything he asked of them and said they would do everything to make the people of the Butana happy. The eldest brother, Ali, then promised his father to rule justly and to look upon his brothers as his father had done. Then Ali said, "Father, you made us break the sticks, then asked us to tie the unbroken sticks together and try to break them. Why was that?"

Their father gave a faint smile. Then with difficulty he said to them, "O my sons! You are like these sticks. If each of you stands alone, by himself, and doesn't pay attention to the others, he will be as easy for an enemy to break as a single stick. But if you band together, and be as the fingers of a hand, you will be unbreakable, just like the bundle of sticks."

THE STORY OF
THE WISE MOTHER

Once upon a time there lived a sultan and his wife. They had only one son. He was called Jalal. Jalal was very smart, strong, courageous, and generous. He grew up and became a kind young man who was loved by everyone.

One day, the sultan fell ill. His son brought many *baseers* who tried many medicines. Every day the illness worsened. One morning the sultan passed away. All the people were sad at the loss of their just leader.

His son, Jalal, became the new sultan. (There is, of course, no Sultan but the creator of the universe.)

His mother said to him, "Oh son, take care! And beware of so-called friends! Most of them will only be looking for your money! So you must choose your friends cautiously and wisely."

The young sultan was astonished. "But how can I do that, mother?" Jalal asked. His mother told him to choose a friend. He chose one of the merchants' sons. They spent time together. The mother then asked her son to invite his friend for breakfast. Jalal did so. The friend came. The sultan's mother delayed the meal until noon. Both of the young men were very hungry. Then she sent them the food. It consisted of only three eggs, nothing else. The friend took one egg. The young sultan took another egg. Each ate his egg. Then the friend took the third egg and gave it to Jalal. The young sultan ate it, and the friend went home. Jalal then went to his mother, who asked him what had happened. When he told her, she advised him not to befriend this young man. She said, "He is a bad person, trying to deceive you into believing that he likes you more than himself. He will take your money." So he left that friend and chose another one.

This new friend was the son of the head of the guards. They became best friends. Wherever one was found the other was there, too.

Again the mother asked her son to invite his friend for breakfast. The friend came. She delayed the meal until noon. Both of them were very hungry.

Three eggs were brought. The friend ate one and Jalal ate one. Then the friend ate the third one and went away. The sultan went to his mother, who asked him about what had happened. He told her.

The mother advised him not to continue being friends with this man, because he was very selfish and if ever he found a chance he would take Jalal's money. She told him to choose a third friend. He looked here and there, but didn't find anyone.

One day, while he was wandering in the forest, he came across a very poor man and his son, who was Jalal's age. The man was a woodcutter. Jalal sat with them. They gave him simple food and some water in a very old pot. The woodcutter's son, who was called Khalid, told Jalal many stories and taught him some tricks. Khalid showed him around the forest and taught him how to cope with it.

The sultan felt great pleasure and happiness, unlike any he had felt before. He began to visit his new friends regularly. Each time he learned more about life, its difficulties, and how to solve those difficulties. The woodcutter's son, Khalid, learned that the young man was the sultan. Khalid said that he was not suited to be the sultan's friend, but the sultan insisted.

Often Jalal and Khalid would play together, and when Jalal went back to his mother he was always dirty. Sometimes he had a cut on his cheek, sometimes he came with a bloody nose, and other times there were wounds on his knees and other places. For some time they went on like that. Then the mother asked her son to invite his friend for breakfast. The same thing happened as before.

When the three eggs were brought to them very late, and they were both hungry, each one took an egg and ate it.

The third egg was left uneaten. Khalid took the third egg, took his knife, and divided it into two. He gave the sultan one half and he took the other half.

After that the woodcutter's son went home. The mother asked her son, the sultan, how the meal went. He told her.

Then she said to him, "This is the true friend. Stay true to him, although he is poor." Jalal followed his mother's advice, and when he and his mother were sure that Khalid was a good, honest, wise young man, the sultan appointed him the prime minister of the sultanate.

They remained good friends ever after.

THE STORY OF
THE WOODCUTTER

A long time ago, a woodcutter and his wife lived in a forest. The woodcutter used to cut wood, sell it in the nearby town, buy what he needed, and come back late in the afternoon. They had a daughter who lived with them. Their house was a small strong house made of wood.

The woodcutter used to wake up at dawn, take his ax, go deep in the forest, and cut wood: kaw, kaw, kaw, tug, tug, tug, chop, chop, chop. When he had cut enough wood, he would tie it with a rope and carry it to the market in the nearby town. He sold the wood to buy food, clothes, and other things for his family.

Into the forest came a very religious man who left behind people, his town, and his family, and came to pray. He wanted to spend the rest of his days worshipping Allah. He was a very good Muslim, who went away from people just to pray for Allah. He was a holy man.

The noise of the woodcutter's ax on the trees—kaw, tug, and chop—disturbed the man and diverted him from his prayers. One day he called the woodcutter. He said to him, "Oh my son, why are you always distracting me with the sound of your ax on the trees?"

The woodcutter said to him, "Oh master! I am a very poor man. I cut the wood, take it to the town market, sell it, and buy what my family and I need."

The man said to him, "I will give you a thing that will satisfy all your needs, and make you not need your work. Take this pot, go home and, when you need anything, say to it, 'Oh my pot! Oh my little pot! Fill yourself with...' and say what you need. The pot will be full of what you want: food, clothes, money, or anything else you desire."

The woodcutter took the pot and went on his way home. On the road he said, "Oh my pot! Oh my little pot! Fill yourself with kings' food." And the pot was full of different kinds of food that he never dreamed of seeing. He ate and went home.

Reaching his house, he told his wife what to do. She ate the best kind of foods with her daughter. They drank the best sort of mild drinks. They were happy and lived that way for months.

One day the woman asked her husband to take the pot to the river and clean it. The woodcutter, taking his pot, went to the river. He found the king's servants washing the king's horses. They asked the woodcutter to come and help them wash the king's horses. He asked them, "How much will you give me?" They told him that they would give him a piaster. He said, "No." They said, "A shilling." He refused. They said, "Ten piasters; two shillings." He said, "All right. I will wash one horse for that money."

He took a horse to the water and said to them, "Hold this pot for me, but don't say to it, 'Oh our pot! Oh our little pot! Fill yourself with food.'" When he was in the middle of the river, washing the horse, the servants put down the pot, sat around it, and said, "Oh our pot! Oh our little pot! Fill yourself with food." The pot filled with food. They ate bread, meat, fruits, and every kind of good food. When the woodcutter came back they hid the pot, refused to give it to him, and beat him severely.

He went home weeping. In the morning he went into the forest with his ax, began to cut wood, and disturbed the holy man again. Kaw, tug, chop, kaw, tug, chop. The holy man asked him again why he made such noise. He told him about the king's servants and what they had done.

This time the holy man gave him a china platter and told him to say to it, "Oh my china platter, give me different foods." The woodcutter took the china platter and walked home. On the road he stopped and said to the platter, "Oh my china platter, give me different foods." It was soon full of bread, fish, chicken, meat, fruit, and many other foods, as well as tea and coffee. He ate, drank, and went home. He told his wife and daughter what to do. They ate and drank. They were all happy. Weeks and months passed and they needed nothing.

About six months later he took the china platter to the river to wash it. There, the king's servants were washing the horses again. They asked him for help. He wanted to know how much they would pay him.

"A pound."

"No."

"Ten pounds."

"No."

"Twenty pounds."

He now agreed, gave them his china platter, and asked them not to say, "Oh our china platter, give us different foods." Taking a horse, he went into the river, to the middle. The servants sat around the platter and said, "Oh our china platter, give us different foods," and it was full of all sorts of foods, sweets, and light drinks. They ate, drank, and were very happy. They hid the platter. When the woodcutter brought the horse out of the river after washing it, he asked for his platter. He was beaten and driven away. He came home weeping. In the morning he took his ax, went into the forest, and began cutting wood. Kaw, tug, chop. Again the holy man called to him and asked what had happened.

The woodcutter told the holy man about the king's servants and what they had done to him and to his china platter.

This time the holy man gave him a heavy club. He told him to take it and say to it, "Oh my club, turn round and round." Before reaching his house, in the middle of the road, as he used to do every time, he stopped and said, "Oh my club, turn round and round."

The club jumped in the air and began to hit and strike him severely. He ran to his wife; the club flew after him and struck him fiercely. He cried and ran, trying to avoid the beating of the club. When he reached his house the club stopped beating him.

He took his club, went to the river, and found the king's servants washing the king's horses.

They asked him to wash a horse for thirty pounds. He accepted and they gave him the money. He took a horse into the river and asked them not to say to the club, "Oh our club, turn round and round."

When he was in the middle of the river, the servants came round the club and said to it, "Oh our club, turn round and round." The club jumped into the air and began to strike them severely. They fell on the ground about to die, but still the club went on striking them. They all cried to the woodcutter to stop the club. He said, "Unless you give me back my pot and my china platter, I'll not let him stop striking you." They gave him the china platter and the pot. Then he said to the club, "Stop that." The club stopped.

The woodcutter took his pot, his platter, and his club and went home.

He and his family were very happy with their things. The daughter grew up into a very pretty young woman. The woodcutter became very rich because of the pot and china platter. He became acquainted with the king and they became dear friends.

The king's son, Prince Taha, became very fond of the woodcutter's daughter and fell in love with her. He married her and they lived happily ever after.

THE GOOD EXCUSE

There was once a king. His name was Jabbar, and he was a very harsh man. His kingdom was very wealthy. He fought against many other kings, and defeated them. Every king feared Jabbar and wanted to be his ally and friend. Many presents were sent to him from other kings—silver, gold, and jewels were styled into sparkling treasures. Day after day the treasure house received more presents of every kind. Statues of men, horses, houses, everything that could be imagined was made in silver and gold, and often had jewels around it. These were the best and most precious presents that were sent to Jabbar.

People feared him. When he thought that a wrong was being done, he killed the offender. Everybody knew that what he did was wrong. But fear tied their tongues, and they could not object. Because nobody argued, he went on doing cruel things. The people wanted to show him that what he did was wrong, in one way or another, but no one dared. Every one of them was numbed by fear.

In a faraway village, people heard of this. Their astonishment at how things happen in other cities and villages made them content with the life they led in their own village. Yet one daring, poor fisherman was not happy about what happened to the people in the king's city. He wanted to stop the king from being so cruel. He was not thinking of making them get rid of their king, but he wanted the king to stop doing so many bad deeds.

The king himself was brave, and made all other kings afraid of

trying to attack his kingdom. In itself, this was a good thing, but being cruel to both his enemies and followers was not necessary. A truly good king would be gentle, loving, and helpful to his people.

The fisherman thought and thought. Every day he thought about this problem. At last he thought that he had a very good solution. The king must be taught how to be good to his countrymen and rough with his enemies. So the fisherman traveled to the king's city. It was not an easy task—he was poor and couldn't afford a camel, a horse, or even a donkey for the journey. He also did not tell anyone in his village about what he was going to do. He took his fishing rod, a box of matches, put on his old rags, and, in the name of Allah, began his good but difficult journey.

He did not leave the banks of the Nile. When he felt hungry, he threw his fishing line in the Nile, and sometimes Allah brought him a fish to satisfy his hunger. Sometimes he did not catch a fish for days, and went on being hungry. But hunger was not a strong enough excuse to make him turn back. The acacia branches and thorns cut his body as he walked. His feet were full of sores and cracks. His face and hands were cut in many places, but those things made him more determined to accomplish what he had put in his mind.

At last, after many days and nights, he arrived at the king's city. He washed his clothes in the Nile, washed himself, and began to think of a way to see the king. He chose a very big shop and went into it. He found a clean, well-groomed man there. The man seemed to be kind-hearted. He approached the man, but did not say a word. He wanted to hear from the man first, and try to learn something from the way the man addressed him.

The man, who was the richest merchant in the city, said to him, "What can I do for you, my son? Do you need food, or clothes, or shelter? How can I help you?"

The fisherman was very pleased by the merchant's words. He said to the merchant, "I am a poor fisherman, from Um Mutala village. I heard of the brave deeds of our king against the country's enemies and was pleased. I heard about our king's cruelty toward us, and was unhappy. I have come all this distance to allow the king to learn how to be kind to us. There is only one thing I wish to do, and that is to make him love his countrymen and treat them as they should be treated. If I fail in that, I shall be killed."

The merchant told the poor fisherman that he would make him the best clothing, so that he would look like a rich man, and would introduce him to the king. The fisherman said that what he was thinking of doing did not need handsome clothes. He must be the servant who brings the food to the king. The merchant agreed and made new clothes for the fisherman to replace his old rags. Then the merchant spoke with the minister, and took the fisherman to his home and waited. The merchant asked him what he planned to do. The fisherman did not tell the merchant. He said, "A long time ago I learned that you are the master of your secret, as long as you keep it to yourself. The moment you tell your secret to others, your secret will be your master. Please allow me to keep my secret to myself until I meet the king. You only need to know the outcome of the secret."

The merchant was quite pleased with the fisherman. He knew that he was in the presence of a wise man. The minister asked the head servant to allow Alim, the fisherman, to be the servant who gives the king his food and drink. Alim was given this post in the palace. He worked well for a long time. He never spoke unless he was spoken to. The king began to like him, because whenever he asked him a question, Alim answered it wisely and completely. The king never needed to ask two questions about a matter. The king came to love Alim very much, and began to tell all his visitors about him.

Now Alim learned that his standing with the king was good, and everybody in the city knew it. The time had come for Alim to do his experiment. He would either die, or the king would see how to treat his obedient followers differently than he treated his enemies. Alim brought a bowl of soup to the king. When he reached the king, he let a drop of the broth fall on the floor. The king's face was now as red as burning coal. He shouted, "Kill him!" That was the chance Alim wanted. When he heard the words of the king, "Kill him," he knew that his time to teach the king had come, so he poured all the broth on the king's clothes and the king was on fire. He asked, "Why did you do that? Silly servant!"

Alim answered in a loud voice, "Because I love you. Everybody near and far away knows that you love your humble servant very much. What will they say when you kill this man, after having told everybody that he is wise and you love him, because a small drop of soup has fallen on the floor? They will say that is not a just king. That is why I poured out all the soup—to give you a good excuse to kill me. Killing me for just a drop of soup on the floor would make all the people say bad things about you. I would not like that. I wanted them to say bad things about me, and say that the king had a good excuse to kill his servant. That is why I poured all the soup on your clothes, to make you find a good excuse, so that people would pardon you for killing me."

It was as if cold water had been poured on the king. Suddenly all his anger disappeared, and he began to think about what Alim had said. He gave another order not to kill him. That was the first time in his whole life that he gave two contradictory orders. From that time on, the poor fisherman was always in the presence of the king, giving wisdom and teaching the king and his ministers. And the king never gave another order, except after thinking it over many times.

(JHERE THE
TREASURE IS HIDDEN

A long time ago, when all the world depended only on planting
and hunting to live, there lived Hannan. Hannan was a young
farmer. He was very strong and faithful. He was also a good hunter,
using the arrow, spear, net, or traps. Hannan had a large plot of land
which he always planted at the rainy season (known in Arabic as *al
Kharief*). Hanna, his mother, lived with him, because her husband,
two sons, and one daughter were dead.

They were very happy together. Hanna was very pleased with her
son Hannan. He never ate before he was sure that she had eaten.
When Hanna was tired, Hannan washed her feet and legs, and at
bedtime he oiled her skin with scented *dihn* oil. In her prayers, Hanna
always said, "Oh, Allah, I am very pleased with my son, Hannan.
Please, Allah, bless him." She was pleased and proud, and always
showed her pride in her son.

There was only one thing that troubled Hanna: she wanted to
bring up her son's children before she died. She talked a lot with
Hannan about this. He was afraid to marry a girl who would not get
along well with his old mother, and serve her. That was why he had
delayed his marriage. When the mother's wish began to be the everyday
talk, Hannan asked her to choose a wife for him. She thought of
choosing a wife who would be willing to live there and serve her.
Hanna chose Safia. Safia was the most beautiful girl in the village.
She was very polite and helpful. So Hannan married Safia. They lived
happily together. Safia looked upon her mother-in-law as a loving mother.

But days, weeks, months, and years passed by without Safia giving birth to a child. Five years passed, and no son or daughter came. Hanna was getting older. She talked with her son, trying to get him to marry a fertile girl who could give birth, but Hannan would not do that, because he saw that the happiness given to him by Safia could not be given by any other woman.

One day, Safia felt a severe pain in her stomach in the early morning. The *baseer* (the healer) was brought. He gave her many medicines. Before the sun set that day, Safia passed away. Hannan was the saddest man in the village.

Two years passed before his old mother could urge him to have another wife. He married Assurra. She was very beautiful, a hard worker, and, moreover, loved both her husband and her mother-in-law. Happiness crept toward that house, after the sadness caused by the death of Safia. Then a strange thing happened to Assurra. Her appetite was not good. Her preference for food was not as it used to be. She always felt sick and often could not keep food in her stomach. Both Hannan and Assurra were in an uneasy state. Assurra began to feel that her end was approaching. Hannan felt the same way. They were very sad.

Strangely enough, Hanna, Hannan's mother, was always smiling and kissing both her son and her daughter-in-law. Though she was too old to work, she didn't allow her daughter-in-law to do any hard work, and was always caring for Assurra. One day, Assurra asked Hanna why she was happy while Assurra was sick and about to die. Hanna said to her that that sickness was not the sort that killed, but the sort that told her that a new baby is coming. Assurra told her husband what his mother had said. Asking his mother, he learned that the illness was what is known as *waham*, the sickness that comes with the first months of pregnancy. He was about to fly with his happiness. The broken tooth in the middle of his bottom row of teeth showed constantly, because he was always smiling. He began to think about bringing up the baby. He decided that the baby should be a boy, his name would be Muhsin, and he would be a strong, generous, brave, learned man.

Months passed. The midwife came, and soon enough, to his greatest happiness, a son was born. The house was full of joy. Men and women came from different parts of the village to congratulate the household. The news traveled far, to different villages where relatives lived. The news was very important, because at that time Hannan was already middle-aged. Presents began to arrive for the child. A poor aunt brought a young she-goat. Another brought a sheep. A third brought a goat and a sheep. Some people brought cows, oxen, and one brought a camel. The richest relative brought one of each kind: a goat, a sheep, a donkey, a horse, and a camel. Muhsin's treasure began to grow.

Muhsin was sent to the *khalwa*, the Qur'an school, at the age of five, and two years later he recited the whole Qur'an by heart and began to learn the sayings of the Prophet. He spent three more years, so that at last he was learning mathematics, languages, and some history. He was now a young man of sixteen years. One of the ladies

said to a friend from another village, "Oh daughter of my mother (this is how Sudanese speak to one another, even if they are not related), if you see him you will feel that he is in his twenties, and the face, oh, the face is just like the moon of fourteen nights. He is as shy as an adolescent girl, always looking at the ground under his feet, although he is very mature. Every girl in his village and the nearby villages wishes to marry him." He was now leading his father and the people of the village in their prayers. He began to help his father on the farm. The farm yielded good crops and his animals increased in number. Although his grandmother, Hanna, had died two years ago, she died happy and smiling. They grieved greatly for their loss.

Three years later, Hannan became ill. The *baseer* came, and was sure that it was nothing serious. But as time went on, he grew worse. One day, Hannan called his son and addressed him. He said, "I feel that I am going to die. I leave you a great treasure under the terrace of the field. When you need it, dig up the terrace." (There are terraces around every field, where the earth is raised to keep the rainwater in the field.) Then Hannan died. All the villagers in the different villages were sad to lose such a fine man. There was a house of mourning for a whole month. People everywhere were sad at the loss of Hannan.

Year after year passed. Muhsin began to lose everything. He was depending on his animals, but a killing disease came and all his animals died, except the old donkey, which had been given to him at his birth. The donkey was now twenty years old, but he could still carry his owner. Muhsin didn't know what to do. One day he remembered his father's words about the treasure hidden under the terrace. There was a great, lofty tree, where his father always used to sit when he rested in the fields. He ate his food under that tree. Muhsin was sure that the treasure was hidden near it. He began to dream about the gold, silver, and money his father had left for him.

Early one morning, just after he did his dawn prayers, Muhsin took his spade, some food, and a small lambskin full of water to the field. He tied his bowl of food and the water skin to a branch of the tree, and began to dig. He thought that he would find the hidden treasure in three or four hours at most. He hoped that he would not need to dig more than ten meters on either side of the tree to find the treasure.

He dug the side toward the east. That took him a long time. Then he began to dig in the opposite direction, toward the west. He dug fifteen meters that way, but did not find anything. There was nothing hidden there. He wondered why his father had not told him the exact location of the hidden treasure, and why he hadn't asked his father. He was certain the treasure would be found near the tree.

The next morning, he came early. He dug fifteen meters before he did his dawn prayers. Then he went on digging, expecting to find the treasure at every step. He dug up the whole southern side of the terrace, and found nothing. Then he turned north and began his work. Days went on. He dug and dug. He dug the entire northern terrace. Then he worked for many more days, and dug the whole eastern terrace. Still he found nothing. So the last side, the western side, must hold the hidden treasure. With great zeal and enthusiasm, he began working on the western side, moving toward the south, where he first began his digging. Muhsin went on digging, and every day he expected to hear his spade hitting an iron box. Only six meters were not dug on that last side of the terrace, but he was very fatigued and exhausted. He went back home, saying to himself, "Tomorrow I will find my treasure."

Muhsin began even earlier the next day, and that part was the most difficult, The ground was like cement. At sunrise, he finished digging the last side of the terrace, but unfortunately there was nothing. Muhsin didn't find the treasure. Maybe it was hidden in the middle of the field, or in one corner or another. "Why didn't my father show me the exact place? Why didn't I ask him about the exact place? Why did he leave it just like this: Go and dig the terrace?" Muhsin went to the nearby village to meet Arrufaie, his father's best friend, to ask him if he knew anything about the treasure. But Arrufaie knew nothing. He asked Muhsin if he had raised the earth. Muhsin told him that he dug very deep, and piled up the earth that made the terrace as high as a wall and very thick. They agreed that, as long as the rain had begun to fall, Muhsin should plant the field, and the following year they would try to find the treasure.

The rains were very heavy. All the terraces of the other people broke in many places, except that thick, high, wall-like terrace of Muhsin.

Every bit of water that dropped in his field stayed there and never went out. The crop was very green and tall. The stalks were healthy and the ears were large. When he harvested this field, Muhsin had more than two hundred sacks of sorghum. He gave the *zakat*, Allah's part, to the poor, sold the greatest part of it, left some for himself and his guests, and he married a beautiful lady.

Arrufaie visited his friend's son at his marriage party. Muhsin asked him when they would look for the hidden treasure. Arrufaie answered, "After I heard of what you had gained from your father's field, I came to believe that the treasure is to raise the terrace that high and thick and plant your father's field. Your father had no treasure except his hard work in the terrace that surrounded the farm. So when he said to you, 'Under the terrace,' he meant that, by digging up the terrace and planting the soil, you would find your treasure. And you have."

HUNTING THE ELEPHANT

They were a band of fifteen men from Shendi town in the northern part of the Sudan. Shendi town lies on the eastern bank of the River Nile. It is a large town. Those fifteen men, who were among the inhabitants of Shendi, used to go to the Dinder River.

The Dinder River came and went. It came in the rainy season in July. At the end of winter, around the last days of February, it disappeared, and only the empty bed remained. But by digging down one foot, people could find water. Those water holes were called *jammamas*. The people and the animals used these *jammamas* until the river flooded again.

The banks of the Dinder River were covered with trees, making a very thick forest that stretched for hundreds of miles. In that forest lived all different types of wild animals—lions, elephants, leopards, hyenas, cheetahs, wolves, wild dogs, zebras, giraffes, and all the different types of gazelles and antelopes. To that band of fifteen Shendi men, the most important animals were the elephants, giraffes, gazelles, and antelopes. Any edible animal was important to them, as they were expert hunters.

They left their town and their families, and traveled that great distance to hunt. They rode on donkey's backs, until they reached Tambool town, or Rufa'a town, sold their donkeys, bought camels, and began their journey toward the Dinder River. There they entered that thick forest. There was a clearing where they had cut the trees many, many years ago. In that clearing, which was called a *taya*, where there were but a few trees, they repaired their old huts or built new ones if the huts had been completely destroyed by the winds. Finishing building their huts, they stretched long ropes between the trees around their huts, to hang the gazelle, antelope, and giraffe meat. They went to the river and filled their *suga*, water skins made of cowhide. After they brought back their *suga* full of water, their *taya* was now ready for the game they would catch.

Every day the hunters went, killed a giraffe or two, many antelopes and gazelles, and sometimes an elephant. Then they went back to the *taya* to retrieve their camels to carry the result of their day's hunt. When they brought back the giraffes, antelopes, and gazelles, they skinned them and cut the meat into long thin strips about three or four feet long. They hung that meat to dry on the ropes they had stretched before. When the meat had dried in that hot sun near the equator, it was cooked, or collected in large sacks. They did not bring the hunted elephants with them to the *taya*, only the ivory. The ivory was put in the hunted animals' hides.

One of the fifteen men was not a hunter at all. He came with them every year just to prepare the food, clean the place, and watch over the drying meat when the others were away hunting more. He made very nice *kissra*, Sudanese bread, and he used the dried meat of the gazelles, giraffes, and antelopes to make the best kind of *mullah sharmut*. When the meat had dried, it was called *sharmut*. When *sharmut* was cooked, it was called *mullah sharmut*.

The *taya* man, who only prepared the food, cleaned the place, and guarded it, knew absolutely nothing about hunting. He had never seen an elephant in his life, dead or alive. He was just in the *taya*. When a dispute happened between him and any of the hunters, he might be called a woman, because he was doing the job of a Sudanese woman, who never did anything except the house jobs—collecting dung for the fire, cooking, washing clothes, cleaning the house, and sleeping in the bed with her husband at night. When a man was called a woman, the result might be murder. No Sudanese man would ever accept being called a woman. He might kill the man who said that.

Although the *taya* man never hunted, he gave advice about hunting. When the hunters began to tell what had happened on that day's hunt, how the elephant was about to kill Omer, or how Ali fell in front of the giraffe, or anything of that sort, he would begin to give his advice. The *taya* man gave advice to Omer on how to avoid the angry, wounded elephant. Having seen no elephant in his life, he always imagined the elephant as large as a dog, and a good tree climber like the leopard. He saw the elephant in place of a leopard. He told Omer that an angry, wounded elephant might be avoided in two ways: if the elephant was high in the branches of the tree, no one should be directly under the tree. One must get away from the trunk of the tree and make a great noise and sounds to make the elephant climb higher and higher. When the elephant was on the highest branch, it must then be shot. When shot and falling from so high, its legs would be broken, and it would not be able to move if it was still alive. If it was still alive, then killing it would be easier, and if it was dead, then that was it. That was how to avoid and kill angry elephants.

The hunters would burst out laughing like thunder. That always made the *taya* man angry and ready to quarrel, but the leader would always cool him down. He told him that they laughed because they never thought of that, which was very easy to do. If Omer did what the *taya* man said, he would not have been in any difficulty or any danger. There, the *taya* man would smile broadly, and walk away toward his kingdom in the kitchen to bring them their meal. He would strut like a turkey.

In the evening, when they had their supper and tea, they listened to the *taya* man's advice and had a hearty laugh over it. Then they went to sleep, and slept until dawn, when they said their dawn prayer and began their day's work.

This usually went on for six months. By that time, they would have collected a good deal of meat, hides, and ivory tusks. They would prepare themselves for their return journey. Four of them would go to Al Guweisi town, to the Rufa'a tribe, to buy camels. Rufa'a tribe had some of the best camels. They would buy the camels they needed, and come back to their *taya*. Three to four days would be spent collecting their elephant tusks and *sharmut*. After that, they would begin their journey from the far southern part of the country to the north.

They came through many towns and villages. In those large markets of the towns, they sold their *sharmut*. When they reached Omdurman and Khartoum, they sold the ivory to the traders who took those things outside the country.

One day, the *taya* man was angry with one of the hunters. They quarreled. The quarrel did not stop as usual. They used their hands as well as their tongues. The *taya* man heard the word "woman" many times; that made him make a very daring decision. He decided that the next day he would not cook, he would go hunting. That day had been set aside especially for elephant hunting.

They had seen the tracks of elephants at a great distance. That was where they would go. The *taya* man told the leader that one of the hunters ought to stay to cook, wash the place, and clean it, because he would not stay, he must go. He would divorce his wife if he couldn't go hunting. The leader refused. A wild discussion broke out. At last the hunters were compelled to agree and accept the *taya* man. They thought that he would add amusement to their hunt, so he was allowed to go. They moved just after dawn. It was a long weary journey for the *taya* man, who had never done it before. Thorns and branches caused him much trouble. The long walk, to which he was not accustomed, played a great part in his displeasure. From time to time, he said to them that of course he had never seen an elephant before. He asked them, the moment they saw an elephant, to tell him. He would hunt it alone, and would show them how to hunt elephants in the best of ways, that they hadn't seen before in their lives. They laughed and agreed to that. Every quarter or half hour, he reminded them that, just when they saw an elephant, he must be told and they must leave the rest of the job to him. He would kill it before it climbed the tree, or entered its hole. They always laughed when he said that.

Hour after hour passed, and they didn't find an elephant. The *taya* man now was weary. He could not raise his legs to walk except with difficulty; he dragged along. He was thirsty, hungry, and fatigued. The earth began to turn round and round under his feet. He was about to fall down, when he saw a hut at a distance. He was very pleased. Would they agree to rest in the shade of that hut, or would the leader urge them to go on? He was not sure. He didn't want to hear the word "woman," if he was the only one who couldn't walk. At last he said to them, "Let us go and rest in that hut." To his astonishment, all of them stopped abruptly. They turned toward him at the same time. He was puzzled about what they did. He knew now that they were all as tired as he was, and didn't want to say so. But now, finding a chance of somebody else mentioning it, they would agree. He was inwardly pleased. They all asked at the same time, "Where is the hut you are talking about?" His pleasure did not allow him to talk. He pointed with the fingers of his right hand in the direction of the hut. They followed his hand, and saw what the *taya* man thought to be a hut. They all said together in a whisper, "That is an elephant!"

The *taya* man couldn't believe his ears. He never thought that there was an animal larger than the wild giraffe or the domestic camel. But, to find an animal larger than a small hut of their *taya*, made his head spin round and round. The sight of that elephant, which he had always imagined climbing trees and entering holes in the ground, made his head spin round and round. Now his legs failed him because of fear. His eyes opened as wide as coffee cups, his mouth opened and dropped, he heaved a great sigh and fell slowly to the ground. The leader told three of the men to carry him to a certain place full of lofty trees and stay with him while the leader went with the others to hunt the elephant. Two men held his legs, and the third held his head; he was a laughable man. They moved on, but the man who was carrying his head began to remember what the *taya* man had said: that when they saw an elephant, they should tell him and leave it to him alone to show them how he would hunt it. When he came to that point, he laughed and laughed. His hands couldn't hold the head, so he let go of the *taya* man's head, and his head fell and hit the ground. That happened time after time. The *taya* man was angry. The other man did not care what happened to him. He was astonished by a hunter who couldn't hold and carry his head. The *taya* man opened his eyes wide, and said to the laughing hunter who was carrying his head, "You, who can't carry and hold my head, why can't you carry a head? We will never bring you to hunt elephants with us again."

I NEED WISDOM
MORE THAN YOU DO

A long time ago, not hundreds of years, but thousands of years ago (although my teacher said it was millions of years ago), there was only one language, which all animals understood and spoke. People were among the animals who understood and spoke that language. Trees, walls, the earth, rivers, everything created by Allah spoke that one language. There was no other language. My grandmother, who told me this story, said to me, "Even things understood and spoke that one language. You must believe and be sure of that. There was no other language but that one. That is why, up until now, we say, 'Walls have ears.'"

There was, at that time, a rich man who had many shops and large tracts of land at different places at Wad Madani city, on the western bank of the Blue Nile. Wad Madani was the second largest city in the Sudan, after the capital. That man, Attahir, was very prosperous, thriving, and successful. All his businesses grew vigorously. Whatever he did brought more wealth. He went on the pilgrimage to Mecca seven times. (As you know, many people save for a lifetime just to go to Mecca once.) Attahir had a large *khalwa* for guests, and every now and then guests came to stay for as long as they needed. They were hosted in the best way a generous Sudanese would show his guests. People who were in need came to him. People who were in need from places near and far came to him, and their needs were always satisfied. Attahir had a fine, strong ox, that used to draw the plow and work hard in the fields. Sometimes the ox was on the *sagia*, a wheel with pots that carries water from the Nile to the canals that water the fields. He worked hard. He was the best animal in all the district. Attahir also had a fine, black donkey. It was a large, beautiful donkey. No donkey could beat him in walking, galloping, or running. He was the pride of the district. Many people brought their she-donkeys to Attahir's donkey, so that they would have the same strong offspring.

In the evening, all the animals of the farm used to meet at one place and talk with each other, or hear stories, or even listen to the strange things that had happened to some of them. The moment they saw a human being, they stopped talking. From long ago, they considered humans to be their masters, and would not share their talking with them. Sometimes, when there was an important matter among the animals, the walls would take what they were talking about and tell it to the humans.

When all the animals went back to their sleeping places, the donkey and the ox would have a special talk that only they two shared. They were considered by all the different animals to be the most senior and special, but every one of them knew that the donkey was a special animal. He was given the best sort of saddle, the fur that was put on the saddle for when the master wanted to ride. He had the most beautiful harness, and was given clover, sorghum, and different types of delicious food. Although the ox was given the same kind of food, everyone knew that the donkey was the most precious one. Only Attahir rode on his back. No one else was allowed to ride on that donkey. He was ridden to houses of marriages to attend the parties, and when they arrived, the donkey was given the best food and clearest water by the hosts. That was why he was the pearl of the farms. Nobody ever dreamed of taking his place. Every animal respected him, talked politely to him, and addressed him as "Sir." He was very proud of that.

He always solved the problems of the different animals, and the disputes among them. When he was not there the ox was always in charge, but the moment the donkey returned, he would reclaim his seniority. The ox knew this and was satisfied. He never thought of taking the donkey's place. That was why they were such good friends, so dear to each other.

One evening, when all the animals went to their homes after visiting with one another, the ox said to the donkey, "I always used to be tired, but now I am more tired and fatigued. I feel that my legs will not carry me, I can't walk. What shall I do?"

It happened that the master was very near, although neither saw him or heard his footsteps. He heard what they were talking about. The ox said, "You are always resting. You only take our master to wedding parties or houses of mourning. You are never tied to the plow, you never work the hard tasks I must handle. What shall I do?"

The master was about to walk away, but he stopped to listen to the donkey's answer. He knew that the donkey was the boss. The donkey answered, "When they bring your supper this evening, don't eat it. Put your mouth on the ground, and tomorrow don't stand up. Pretend you are sick." The master, hearing the conversation, walked slowly to his house.

In the early morning, the farmhand who was responsible for the ox and the plowing came to the master and said, "I found all the supper of the ox as I put it last night. The ox tasted nothing of it. When I tried to make him stand up, he refused. He couldn't. I think that he is very ill, and needs to go to the *baseer*, the healer, or we need to bring the *baseer* here to him."

The master answered, "Leave the ox now. Take my donkey and let him do the work of the ox."

The farmhand was astonished. The donkey? The precious mule of the farm? He would never have thought of that! Have the precious donkey do the hard work of the ox? That was unbelievable. He went and took the donkey from his stall. The donkey was very pleased. He thought that his master was going on an important journey. But he was taken to where the plow waited for him. He was put to the plow, and began doing the work of the ox. It was a very difficult job, and he felt about to die. He worked, and worked, and worked, and worked, from dawn to sunset. He was given no food, no water, no shade in which to rest. He just worked, and worked, and worked, first in one place, then another, then another. There was no rest at all. He was covered in sweat. That day was hell for him. "How can I bear all this work? I was not created for this work. What shall I do tomorrow, and the days after that, if the ox goes on pretending he is sick? What will happen to me if the ox goes on doing what I have told him to do? This was my mistake. I must find a way to make him return to his work, or I shall die."

At sunset he was brought home. He was in the worst condition. He was hungry, thirsty, and tired. He was even out of breath. He could not stand up, so he lay down, about to die. After some time, he gained a little strength. Now he began to think about his problem. How could he solve his sad and difficult perplexity? If the ox did not begin his work tomorrow, the donkey would die.

All the animals came. They had their problems and questions waiting for solutions. The donkey asked the ox to answer for him. The ox had been resting all day, and his mind was sharp. He gave the best answers. In the end, when all the animals went away, in the dead of night, the master came and hid near them. The ox asked the donkey, "How did you spend your day? I had the best rest I ever had. I enjoyed every minute of it, and ate all the food that was brought to me. Life is very good now. I like it. How did you spend your time, how was your day? Why do I see you so sad?"

The donkey answered, "That was my best day. I took my master to a friend of his who has a garden. It was full of fruit. I tasted some fruits for the first time in my life. I enjoyed all my time, every minute of it was paradise to me. That man was the best friend of our master. From him, we visited another friend, his friend the butcher, you know. He is a fat man, with cheeks like balloons and a large stomach. I did not like his language. It was all about killing, slaying, skinning, and cutting and breaking bones." He went on speaking like this. "Then I heard the worst news about you. That is why I am now sad."

The ox was afraid. He asked, "What have you heard about me? What is the bad news?"

The donkey said, "My master told the butcher that his ox is of no use now. He doesn't pull the plow. He just lies down and eats, he gives nothing, he takes everything. My master said he wants to sell his ox. The butcher said, 'I need an ox to slay tomorrow. I have no ox for tomorrow. All my animals are just sheep. Some people like ox meat. So I can buy the ox from you.' But my master said, 'I shall see tomorrow.

If I see tonight that the ox did not eat his food, and if tomorrow he cannot do his work, then he will be yours.' The butcher said, 'I need the ox very much, I want to slay it tomorrow, for people need the meat.' Then the master smiled and left."

The ox was in no easy mood. When the grass was brought, he ate it all. In the morning he was standing up before the farmhand came. He went to his plow. The donkey said to himself, "Advice does not always bring good results to the advisor. I needed the advice for myself before I gave it to the ox. That advice nearly killed me."

NO RATS IN THE HOUSE

O nce upon a time, there was a prosperous sultanate where all the
people lived very happily. The sultan was kind and just. The
people were treated in the best way, just as they wanted to be treated.
Everything was going as everybody liked.

Whenever anybody needed anything, he or she would go to the
sultan and ask for help. The sultan would soon do what the people wanted.
So, life went on smoothly and well. The sultan was loved by everyone.

In his town, there was a happy family. The father was kind and
loving to his wise wife, his children, and the townspeople. He was
loved by all the people of the town. He was known to be brave,
generous, courageous, and a learned, wise man. He was very happy
because he had good, clever children, and a very pretty and smart
wife. She tried her best to bring up her children in the best ways.
Their children were healthy and seemed to have all the good virtues
of both their parents. Everybody in the town wanted their children to
be like the children of those two parents. Life was paradise for them.
They were happy and satisfied. Every day that passed brought more
happiness to their house. Things went on like that for years.

One day the father fell ill. All the medicines of all the *baseers* were
of no use. Sadness was felt by everybody in that happy house. Then
the father passed away. Not only his family, but all the people of the
town—men, women, and children—were sad at the loss. He seemed
to be the man of the town. His wise wife was the saddest woman
for months and years to come. Known for her kindness, beauty,

and wisdom, many men asked her to marry them. But she refused. She spent her time bringing up her children and remembering her late husband. She went on living with her children, using whatever money her husband had left them.

The boys grew up. They became young men. The girls grew up. They became young women. The young men married, and the young women married, and all of them built their own homes and went to live in them. Their mother went on living by herself.

Time passed, and her fortune began to shrink. Day after day, her money was spent for life's necessities. Little by little, the money passed between her fingers. It was spent wisely. Every piaster was spent in the right place, and she had no extravagance. The money was spent wisely, but piaster after piaster went away without one single piaster coming in its place. In the course of time, not a single piaster was left. The woman thought of different ways to get more money for her everyday needs. No one must know what had happened. She tried her best so that no one would notice the loss of her money and her need, especially her children.

Her jewelry began to disappear: she had to sell it for money to spend on daily needs. This went on for months and years. Then the gold and silver disappeared. Things began to disappear from the house—then the clothes. At last, nothing was left for her. She began to think of asking her children. She thought of visiting them and telling them about her situation. But she thought that another way of solving her problem would be better. She thought of visiting the sultan and asking him for help.

She wore what was left of her best clothes, and went to the sultan's palace. Outside the palace she found the guards, and asked to obtain permission to see the sultan. One of the guards went in and gave the woman's name and request to the sultan. The sultan knew her, and he allowed her into his presence. Entering the palace, she was led to the sultan. She was very happy, thinking that all her problems would be solved. She was about to fly with pleasure.

But when she entered the room, she found it full of the important people of the city. To her displeasure, they were not going to leave the palace any time soon, as they were deep in discussion with the sultan.

She was shy, and couldn't make her request to the sultan in front of these people. The sultan was pleased to see her, and was more pleased to help her, if she needed any help. She must think of a way to tell the sultan of her problem, without the important people hearing from her own lips that she was in need. Some of them had asked her hand in marriage when her husband died, and she had refused them. She thought they might feel that, if she had married them, she would have no problem. The sultan welcomed her warmly, and talked to her politely about different things. At last, he asked her, "Do you have any problem? What do you need? What can I do for you? What is it that you want?"

The woman looked at the ground under her feet. She knew that the sultan was good, just, smart, and very clever. She wanted to find a way to tell him about her problem indirectly, so that he could understand it without the other people knowing about it.

"What is your problem?" he asked again.

The woman, still looking at the ground under her feet, said to him, "My problem, O sultan, is that all the rats and mice have disappeared from my house. Not a single rat is to be seen in the house. All the rats and mice have left my house."

The sultan smiled and said to her, "Go home now. Your house will have all the rats and mice that disappeared."

After she left, the people around the sultan spoke of their astonishment at a woman who wanted rats in her house. Every one of them wanted to get rid of the rats and mice in their houses, and were ready to pay to do so. What was the matter with the woman? Was she mad?

The sultan said that she was not mad. He told them that the woman was shy, polite, and smart. She did not want to tell her problem and have everyone know it. Having no rats, having no mice in her house, meant that she was bankrupt. She didn't have the things that make rats and mice interested in a house. No cheese, no butter, no bread, none of those little things that make rats and mice live. The sultan told them that a house with no rats or mice meant that there was no food in it.

After that, her house was full of rats and mice.

PLANT WELL,
CULTIVATE WELL

A long time ago, about three hundred years ago, there lived a husband and a wife. They were farmers. They planted their farm in the rainy season (in Arabic it is called *al Kharief*), looked after it, and when the crop was ripe they harvested it. They used to work together.

Every morning, before sunrise, Naeema, the wife, woke up, said her prayers, took her palm leaf basket, and went out. She would collect a great amount of cattle dung for the fire. Most times she would collect half a basket full of the dung, although sometimes she would return home with her basket full to the brim. She would go to her neighbor, bring a small, burning piece of charcoal, put it under the *kanoon*, a small stove for cooking food, and surround it with dung. Kneeling on the ground and putting her hands down to rest on them, Naeema would take in a deep breath, then blow gently. Her mouth would be very near the dung, where she had put the burning piece of charcoal. She would breathe in, and bring the fresh air through her mouth to the charcoal and dung. This helped the charcoal to burn and catch the dung on fire. She cooked everything in the dung fire.

Naeema was always tired and asked herself why she had not married a rich man who could get her a servant to help her do everything at home. Every day she talked to herself about this. She decided that Majdoub, her husband, would not be able to live without her. Naeema began to neglect Majdoub's needs. She didn't cook until very late. When Majdoub asked for tea for his friends,

Naeema pretended she didn't hear. His bed was not made. The tears in his clothes were not sewn or mended. His poor house, which he had looked upon as paradise, now became hell. He used to spend most of his time at home. Now he began to spend his time away from home, away from Naeema. Majdoub began to spend most of his time with his mother and his friends. He came home late, when he was sure that his wife was asleep. When they met, he did not talk to her. He ate her food no more. He neglected her as she did him. He neglected her completely.

Naeema now knew that she had gone too far in her game against her husband. She went to a wise, learned man who was known all over the country, who could solve any and every problem. She told him her situation. He asked many questions, and received many answers. He knew the whole problem. He could solve it. He said to her, "Slay a sheep, divide it into three parts. Keep two thirds at home, and bring the last third to me when you are ready." Three days later, she visited the wise man, carrying one third of the sheep. He said to her, "Go to the forest. Near the large acacia tree, there you will see a lion. Throw the sheep meat to him, and stay back, where he can see you, but don't get too near. When you do that, and the lion eats all the meat, come to me."

Naeema went to the forest. Near the acacia tree, she saw a very fearful lion. His mane covered his eyes; his body was as large as a horse. She put the piece of meat in front of him, and stood back. The lion moved slowly toward the sheep, and ate the meat. He looked at Naeema in a thankful way. Naeema returned to the wise man, and told him the whole story. He was very pleased, and told her to bring the second third the next day.

When she came the next day, the wise man said to her, "Go to where you went yesterday. Give the lion this meat. Sit near him while he is eating, and stroke his body and his head, and be kind in every way." She went to the forest, found the lion, put the piece of meat at his feet, and sat near him. He began to eat. She began stroking his head and his body, kneeling near him. He was very gentle with her. He didn't do anything but eat. When he finished eating, he leaned his whole body on hers, and licked her hand. She was pleased.

She went back to the wise man and told him what had happened. The wise man was very pleased. Everything went as he had imagined. Now he said to her, "Tomorrow, take the last portion of the meat, go to the lion, give it to him, sit near him, stroke his head and body, then pull out one of his whiskers."

Naeema went to the forest, gave the lion the piece of meat, and sat near him. When the lion began to eat, Naeema stroked his body, his head, and pulled a whisker from his upper lip. Nothing happened. The lion did not do anything to Naeema. She went back to the wise man, told him what had happened, and gave him the whisker. He said to her, "You were good to the lion, who did not have any relationship to you, and he let you pull a whisker from his upper lip. What do you think you could do to your husband, if you are good to him? If you are good to your husband, you will find his love and his friendship again."

And in that moment was born the Sudanese proverb, "One who is kind can pull out a lion's whisker."

THE RIGHT DEED AT THE RIGHT TIME

The people of the village lived happily all the time. They needed nothing that they did not have. The Nile flooded in the autumn (known in Arabic as *al Kharief*), and brought a lot of silt, which was always fresh and fertile. After the flood, the river began slowly to withdraw, leaving the most fertile earth. Whenever the river withdrew a yard, two yards, less than that or more, the people planted the land. When the Nile returned to its normal course, and began its journey northward, all the plantations on both sides of the banks were green and lovely to look at. The plants were healthy and strong. Only the sandy places, which were enriched with dung or manure, were the best for the watermelons, sorghum, and all that they needed from plants. The people also had their cattle, which gave them milk, butter, cheese, and even hides. As for meat, they had a lot of goats and a good number of sheep. Their pride was their hens and cocks. They had hundreds of hens, which produced the largest and best sort of eggs. They also took great pride in their cocks, especially in one big, beautiful cock. He was very strong. He was fearless. He did not fear even the foxes. He made the most beautiful sound, which awakened the village people at dawn for their prayer and the beginning of their daily work. That cock was called Antar. "Antar" had been the name of a famous strong black warrior and poet in Arabia before the time of the Prophet. That period was, and is still, called *Jahiliya*. So Antar was known to be the strongest, most fearless, and the bravest fighter of his time.

There was a thick forest, full of different animals, but the foxes were the most dangerous enemies of the village. Before Antar was born, those Abul Husseins (as foxes are affectionately called, for their ability to be sly tricksters) used to visit the village every night and kill and eat many hens. Things changed after Antar grew up. He was fearless. When Abul Hussein came, Antar would make all his feathers stand on end, open his large beak, make ready his sharp claws, and attack. No Abul Hussein could face him. That is why all the foxes feared going to the village, and were satisfied with what they found in the forest. There were many rabbits, rats, mice, and different insects that satisfied their hunger.

A certain Abul Hussein was always hungry for the hens, especially the hens of Antar's village, so he always tried to steal a hen and run away with it before Antar could find out. But Abul Hussein always failed. Day after day, and night after night, he thought of eating a fat hen, but every attempt failed. Antar was there doing his best and being a faithful knight and savior of all the hens and other cocks.

Now Abul Hussein began to think, and think some more, and think yet more and more. All his thinking did not do any good. All he wanted to do was to cause catastrophes for various animals and people. He was very selfish. He thought of nothing but himself. Those things that would bring him the greatest pleasure he would gladly do even if they caused the worst to happen to others. All he thought about was how to be able to eat a hen or a cock every day from that special village, without having any trouble with Antar. Abul Hussein once went to the village by daylight, at the time when all the people were taking their mid-day rest. He stood a good distance from Antar, and asked Antar to befriend him. Antar said, "There are many foxes in the forest who would be happy to be your friend. There are many hens and cocks in the village who will be happy to befriend me. You are in no need of my friendship, and I am in no need of yours, because birds of a feather flock together. You only want an excuse to come to the village to steal the hens. You better go now, or you will regret having come here." And with that, Antar made his feathers stand on end, opened his beak, and charged. Abul Hussein found that the best thing for him was to retreat and run to the forest, so he did that.

His thinking never stopped. Now he decided to get rid of Antar, to kill Antar himself. Then he would have the pleasure of eating the village hens. Abul Hussein tried to learn everything about the village, the hens, and Antar. He disguised himself many times, went to the village, and listened. He learned that all of the people were fond of Antar's voice. All the hens and cocks were pleased by his voice, too. Antar himself was pleased and proud of his voice. Abul Hussein learned that Antar's voice was his weak spot. That was it. The fox thought that he could win his battle against Antar through his voice. He made many plans to do so. If one of them failed, another would succeed. He began to study them, to turn them over and over in his mind. At last, he cooked up a plot against Antar.

He visited the village, and called to Antar that he had come for good, not evil. Antar did not believe that, but he didn't realize that he should not listen to the wicked Abul Hussein. Abul Hussein said to Antar, "I tried my best to deceive you and kill the hens, but frankly you were very brave and clever, and I was no match for you. I will not deny this. But recently I heard rumors in the far forest about your voice. Every animal told me that you have the best voice. Even the doves who have the best voices said that. I do not believe that, but nice voices are my pleasure. Could I hear you? Sing one song only once, and I promise you that we shall never see each other again."

Antar was very pleased. He said, "Do the animals of the forest really talk about my voice? Is it true that they say things about my nice voice?"

The fox answered in the affirmative, saying, "They speak of it all the time."

Antar was very proud. He came very near Abul Hussein, closed his eyes, opened his mouth... and he was caught by the neck! The fox opened an ugly mouth full of sharp white teeth, and caught Antar by the neck. He began to drag him toward the forest. Antar knew he had been tricked. He was very sad, but he was thinking. Fortunately, they came near a village between Antar's village and the forest. Many dogs barked and howled at Abul Hussein. Some of them ran after him. Antar saw that this was a good chance for his escape, but the dogs were not very keen and the fox doubled his pace. Before losing his chance,

Antar said to the fox, "I know them. If you want to get rid of these dogs, tell them that the cock is not from their village. Say that to them. Tell them that the cock is from another village, and they will let you go."

Abul Hussein believed that, and was very pleased. He opened his mouth to speak to the dogs. When he opened his mouth, he let go of Antar, who dropped to the ground. Antar let his feathers stand on end, opened his beak, and was ready for attack, but Abul Hussein did not even stop to look. He was running for his life. The dogs were pursuing him zealously and with great enthusiasm. Losing the cock and the village hens, the fox said to himself, "If I did not open my mouth, as Antar had told me, I could have eaten him and then eaten the village hens. Unlucky is the mouth that opens at the wrong time."

Antar reached his village safely. All the other hens and cocks were pleased to see him again among them. He began to think about how the fox had been able to deceive him and catch him. He remembered that when he believed Abul Hussein, when he asked him to sing, Antar shut his eyes to sing. He did not see the fox attack. So, closing his eyes was the cause of his being caught. That was a silly thing to do. Antar said, "Allah curses those eyes that close at the wrong time." And Abul Hussein said, "Allah curses the mouth that opens at the wrong time." And so came the right deed at the right time.

A FAIR PRICE

He was very fat. From shoulder to thighs, he was exactly like a barrel. That was why all the people of the town called him Barrel. He did not mind his new name, because the name that was given to him on the seventh day after his birth, after his father had slain two fat sheep, was Miser. So he always thought that the name Barrel was far better than the name Miser. He always told his only friend that his name, Barrel, was better than his name Miser. His friend always corrected him. He said, "There is no good or better or best in your names. Don't say, 'My name Barrel is better than my name Miser,' because both of your names are bad. Will you please try to remember that?"

"But what shall I say then?" Barrel asked his friend.

The friend answered, "Say 'I am pleased with the name Barrel, because the name Miser is worse than the name Barrel.' You see, Barrel and Miser are both bad, and you can't say 'My name Barrel is better.' Always say, 'My name Miser is worse.'"

"Oh, I see, I understand now." But he never saw. And he never understood. Because he continued to say, "My name Barrel is better than my name Miser." The two friends frequently talked about the two names. It was the only topic the two friends discussed. They had no other topic of conversation.

Barrel loved money. He worshipped every piaster that found its way to him. The piaster that got to him would never be free again, and move from hand to hand as it had once done. It would never come out again. Barrel was always the final destination of any piaster. He was a piaster grave.

Barrel's cheeks were like the balloons with which the children played. People always said that he had an apple in each cheek; they were always red. His mouth was always working. It never stopped. There was always something between his teeth. He was always eating. There were always peanuts, pieces of cooked potatoes, or a piece of meat in his mouth. It was said that his mouth was like a grain mill—it went on working and working and working. The largest gourd would be nothing compared to his stomach. When he walked his stomach moved in the most curious way. It moved up, down, and from side to side. The children always laughed at it, and pointed at Barrel's stomach.

Barrel's manners were the worst in the town. He was always quarrelsome, especially in matters of money. He could quarrel with his father for the smallest piece of money, for one milim, one tenth of a piaster. He would do anything that brought a small piaster to him, right or wrong. He never cared. He wanted the piaster to be his. The important question was: Will more money come to me as a result? Will this end in more money coming to me? Barrel would act according to the answer.

Miskeen was the poorest man in that town. He was very thin. He couldn't do any heavy work because of continuous illness. His continuous illness took all his strength, especially the malaria. Malaria was Miskeen's permanent friend. It never left him for a full fortnight. Miskeen always shivered because of the malaria. When he walked, his legs shook under him. Everyone watching Miskeen walk thought that he would fall with the next step. They thought that the next step he took would bring him to the ground. They wondered how he was still alive. Miskeen depended on what he was given by good people when he had done a very small job for them. Miskeen was the worst enemy of Barrel/Miser, because not a single piaster came to Barrel through the hands of Miskeen.

Sometimes, Miskeen would ask Barrel/Miser for some food from his kitchen. Miskeen would stand outside Miser's place and look at the hundreds of townspeople sitting around the many tables. The servants went from table to table giving the people different kinds of food.

When Miser was not looking, or when he was inside, Miskeen would walk quickly between the tables that the people had left, and he would collect what was left of their meals. He did that as quickly as possible, so as not to be caught by Miser. Sometimes he would find himself face to face with Miser. He would be collecting the leftover food, and Miser would come up slowly behind him. When he reached him, he snatched what Miskeen had collected, took him in his strong hands like a little stick, and threw him into the street. Sometimes hours would pass without Miskeen being able to stand up again or raise himself up. He kept trying to find out why Miser hated him so much. He couldn't find an answer. He wondered why Miser did not allow him to take the leftover food, even though Miser threw it all away.

One day, a very strange thing happened between the two men. The baker gave Miskeen a loaf. Miskeen didn't find anything to eat his loaf with—no eggs, no milk, no food of any kind. He carried his loaf, and came across Miser's kitchen. There was the very nice aroma of meat being cooked. Miskeen inhaled deeply. He sat down and began to eat his loaf, accompanied by that aroma. It was very nice. He enjoyed his meal, which contained a piece of bread and the fragrance of the food. Miser was looking fiercely at Miskeen. When the loaf was finished, and Miskeen was about to leave for his midday nap under a tree or in the shade of a house, he was caught by Miser. Miser took him inside his place, inside his room. He ordered him to pay. Miser wanted Miskeen to pay for the aroma with which he had eaten his loaf. But Miskeen had eaten nothing, and refused to pay for nothing. Their cries rose. The sheikh's guard came along the road. The sheikh's guard was the lawman. He heard the two people crying and shouting. He entered the kitchen to see what was the matter. He was told by Miser that Miskeen didn't pay. Miskeen told the guard that he had taken nothing to pay for. But Miser told the guard that Miskeen had eaten his loaf with the aroma of Miser's good food, and he must pay. "I must be paid for the aroma of my food."

The guard took out a piaster from his pocket, and showed it to both men. Miser was very pleased, knowing that the guard was now willing to pay for Miskeen's meal, which consisted of the aroma. He prepared his answer to the question he thought the guard would ask.

He thought the question would be, "How much are you asking Miskeen?" He would answer, "A piaster," and then he would be given the piaster. He was very pleased, and smiled inwardly. Secretly, he felt that he was beginning to like Miskeen a little, he was just beginning to like him. Wasn't he going to make him receive the piaster of the guard? While Miser was thinking these thoughts, the guard said, "Look carefully and listen carefully, Miser." Miser looked at the piaster very carefully. The guard threw the piaster on the table in Miser's room. The piaster danced across the table, and moved from one side to the other. All of them watched the piaster's movement from side to side, and heard the nice music of the singing of the piaster.

When at last the piaster stopped moving, the guard asked Miser, "Did you see the movement of the piaster? Did you hear it singing?"

"Yes," answered Miser. "I have both seen the piaster and heard it singing."

The guard said, "Looking at the piaster and hearing its song are a fair price for enjoying the aroma of your cooking. Now you have been paid in full."

Other Titles in the Series

Children of Wax
African Folk Tales

collected and written by Alexander McCall Smith

"A treasure trove for all those who value folk literature presented with respect and scrupulous care."

—*Kirkus Reviews*

The 27 stories collected from the Ndebele people of Zimbabwe demonstrate the wealth and variety of traditional African folk tales.

ISBN 1-56656-314-3 • $11.95 pb • 128 pages

Imagining Women
Fujian Folk Tales

selected and translated by Karen Gernant

"These stories are all entertaining... rich in cultural significance... a welcome addition to anyone's library who has enjoyed Maxine Hong Kingston and Amy Tan... Karen Gernant's translation doesn't miss a step in opening up this culture to an American audience..."

—*Small Press Review*

ISBN 1-56656-173-6 • $29.95 hb
ISBN 1-56656-174-4 • $14.95 pb • 288 pages

The Grandfathers Speak
Native American Fok Tales
of the Lenapé People
collected and written by
Hitakonanulaxk (Tree Beard)

"The importance of this well-researched work lies in its recording of the Lénape legends, which have been gathered and presented here in their entirety for the first time... Recommended..."
—*Library Journal*

ISBN 1-56656-129-9 • $24.95 hb
ISBN 1-56656-128-0 • $11.95 pb • 160 pages

The Sun Maiden
and the Crescent Moon
Siberian Folk Tales
collected and translated by James Riordan

"The book is a fascinating introduction to the oral literature of Siberia's diverse people and is recommended to folklorists, cultural historians, and general readers..."
—*Small Press*

ISBN 0-940793-66-0 • $24.95 hb
ISBN 0-940793-65-2 • $11.95 pb • 224 pages

Russian Gypsy Tales
translated by James Riordan
collected by Y. Druts and A. Gessler

"A grand collection... The stories are splendid... As a collection of gypsy folklore, this seems to be unique; for readers or storytellers, it's a treasure trove."
—*Kirkus Reviews*

"Compelling... An unusual and substantial volume."
—*Publishers Weekly*

ISBN 0-940793-97-0 • $11.95 pb • 160 pages

The Demon Slayers and Other Stories
Bengali Folk Tales
collected and written by Sayantani DasGupta and Shamita Das Dasgupta

The 20 tales and nine poems in this anthology give the reader a fascinating insight into the oral literature and rich culture of Bengal, the region now comprising of West Bengal in India, and Bangladesh.

ISBN 1-56656-164-7 • $24.95 hb
ISBN 1-56656-156-6 • $12.95 pb • 224 pages

Tales of the Seal People
Scottish Folk Tales
by Duncan Williamson
Winner of the Anne Izard Storytellers'
Choice Award

"... the greatest living English-speaking
storyteller."
—Storytelling Festival

A collection of 14 selkie (half-seal, half-human
creatures) tales from the Orkney and Shetland
islands off the northern tip of Scotland.

ISBN 1-56656-101-9 • $24.95 hb
ISBN 1-940793-99-7 • $11.95 pb • 160 pages

The Snake Prince and Other Stories
Burmese Folk Tales
collected and retold by Edna Ledgard

The people of Burma/Myanmar call it
Shwe Pyidaw, the Golden Land, their fertile
valley cradled in a horseshoe of mountains.
When squabbling Western nations vied for
control of the newly-mapped country a century
ago, the local population had already lived in
the mountainous land for over a millenium.
Throughout those centuries, the legends and tales rooted in animist
religions created a rich tapestry of spirits that underlie the later arrival
of Buddhism. This volume brings together 25 of the most-loved of these
folk tales.

ISBN 1-56656-313-5 • $15.00 pb • 224 pages